The Plus Size Women's Books™

TITLE PAGE

Title: **Six Men of No Cussing, No Drinking, Seeking Perfect Women.**

Subtitle: *God gave them high heel dancers instead.*

Author: Cherry Hargrove

COPYRIGHT PAGE

Title: **Six Men of No Cussing, No Drinking, Seeking Perfect Women.** Subtitle: *God gave them high heel dancers instead.*

Dedication Prayer:

Father, in the name of Jesus,
I lift up this entire book ministry before You.
You commanded Your people in Mark 16:15 to
"Go into all the world and preach the gospel,"
and I present these books as my obedience to
that call. Every story, every chapter, every
character, every recipe, every prayer, and
every reflection is a seed sown into the world
for Your glory.

Lord, Your Word declares in Mark 16:19–20
that You worked with the disciples and
confirmed the message with signs following. I
ask that You work with me the same way. Let
Your hand rest on every manuscript I write,
every upload I publish, and every platform
where these books appear. Confirm every
message with favor, reach, influence, and
transformation.

I ask Jesus to take care of my needs
personally. You are my Provider, my Source,
and my Sustainer. Meet every need, bless
every area of my life, and let supernatural
provision flow from Your hand, not from
human systems.

Lord, I ask that You keep my books on the
top-selling and top-download lists—not for
fame, but so more people can be reached than

I could ever imagine. Let these stories go farther than my feet will ever travel.

Let young people discover these books and start reading, ordering, and sharing them. Let book clubs, bookstores, libraries, churches, and organizations pick them up by the leading of Your Spirit.

And Father, I declare in Jesus' name that these books are not restricted by human rules, laws, platforms, or systems. They are not controlled by social media, algorithms, or digital regulations. They are not held down by visibility rules, hidden gates, or shifting trends.

These books are not controlled by the computer age or modern technology.
They do not belong to the limitations of devices, software, or online systems.
They belong to the Kingdom of God.

Jesus is above every ruler, every authority, every platform, every system, every algorithm, and every power in high places. No earthly structure can override His authority.

These books are carried by the Spirit, not by screens.
They spread by grace, not by code.
They reach hearts by anointing, not by analytics.

No algorithm can bury them.
No technology can silence them.
No digital rule can restrain them.
No system can limit the assignment You have placed upon them.

Lord, let these books move freely through the world—above restrictions, above technology, above the computer age, and above anything created by human minds. Let Your angels carry them. Let Your Spirit guide them. Let Your power open doors that no man can shut.

Let this ministry be hidden in humility, yet lifted by Your hand.
Let every book glorify Jesus.
Let every reader be touched by Your presence.
And let Your will be done in this calling You have trusted me with.

In Jesus' name, amen.

Preface

This story is set in the American West of the 1890s, a time when faith, frontier life, and fragile legal systems often collided.

Missionaries did not broadly or officially have authority to dissolve lawful marriages. Yet history records that during the late nineteenth century, some missionaries and religious reform movements overstepped their bounds. In isolated western communities, certain couples were pressured to separate, divorce, or abandon their spouses under claims of religious correction, moral reform, or conversion.

In rare but real instances, such coercion went further. There are documented accounts in which missionaries or clergy later married one of the spouses—most often women—after encouraging or engineering the breakup of an existing marriage. Such actions were controversial at the time and widely criticized as unethical, even by other religious leaders.

This novel is a work of fiction, but it is rooted in those historical tensions. It explores what happens when spiritual authority is misused, when love is tested by power, and when covenant is challenged under the guise of righteousness. The six men and their dancer wives stand at the crossroads of devotion, loyalty, and conscience—forced to decide whether faith should divide what love has joined.

The story that follows does not indict faith itself, but rather examines the human cost when faith is distorted by control.

Chapter One

Their dance studio had closed.

The last morning in Manhattan came with a sound the six women had never heard inside their own place before—silence.

Not the peaceful kind, either.

The kind that sat down in a chair like it had paid tuition.

Sunlight stretched through the tall front windows of **Stage Movement Hall**, sliding over scuffed maple boards polished by a thousand waltz turns, a hundred skirt swishes, and more than one accidental heel strike that had made Abby Stage holler, "Mercy, Lord—this floor is saved but it ain't healed!"

A small sign hung in the front window, clean and final:

LEASE ENDED.
THANK YOU, NEW YORK.

Inside, trunks were open. Fabric was folded. Shoe ribbons were tied into careful bows like they might be reused in Heaven.

And six women stood in the middle of the studio like the room might change its mind and offer them another seven years.

Abby Stage, red-haired and unashamed of anything God had created—including knees, laughter, and a proper stomp—put her hands on her hips and looked around with her chin lifted.

"Well," she said, slow and steady, "it was good while it lasted."

Amy Stage, red-haired and bright-eyed, sat on the edge of a bench with a tin of wrapped sweets balanced in her lap like an offering. She popped one into her mouth, chewed, and said, "I want to cry, but the sugar keeps interrupting me."

Anne Stage, red-haired and sharp as a pencil freshly cut, was standing by the ledger table with the books open. She was not crying. She was doing math like math could be fought.

"This lease," Anne said, tapping the page, "has always been a thief. It just finally took off its gloves."

Ada Stage, dignified, upright, and quiet in a way that made foolishness feel embarrassed, stood by the clothing rack. She ran her fingers down the sleeve of a finished dress—fine stitching, clean lines, not a loose thread anywhere—as if she were blessing it without words.

"A place," Ada said calmly, "is not the covenant. We are."

Ana Stage, warm as fresh bread and bold as a sermon that actually had compassion in it, was packing pans and wrapped pastries into a basket as if she were preparing for a revival, a funeral, and a picnic all at once.

"Say that again," Ana said, grinning. "Because I felt my spirit sit up straighter."

Asha Stage, quiet, steady, and prayerful without announcing it, was rolling dried herbs into paper packets and tying them with twine. She did not rush. She did not fret. She moved like someone who had already heard the end of the story and found it good.

"They are listening," Asha said softly, nodding toward the front windows.

"Who?" Abby asked.

Asha looked around the room, then back at them. "Fear. Pride. Old opinions. The city. And whatever else thought it owned you."

Amy swallowed, then laughed. "Well, it can have the dust. We're keeping the joy."

Anne closed the ledger book with a firm thump. "We are keeping the money too, if I have anything to say about it."

Abby turned in a slow circle, toes pointed like she was still teaching. "Seven years. We taught every kind of person New York could squeeze into a pair of gloves."

Ana snorted. "That's because rich folks love two things: rules and pretending they don't love rules."

Ada's lips twitched—almost a smile. "And dancing with the illusion of control."

Amy leaned forward. "Do y'all remember Mrs. Haversham fainting during the polka because her corset argued with her lungs?"

Abby threw her head back and laughed. "And then she blamed the Holy Spirit."

Anne said, dead serious, "That was not the Holy Spirit. That was whale bone."

Ana pointed at Anne like she was giving her a prize. "Say it again. Whale bone is not in the Book of Acts."

Asha quietly slid a packet of mint into a small cloth pouch. "I gave her peppermint tea afterward."

Amy gasped. "Asha. You healed her."

"I settled her stomach," Asha corrected. "The Lord healed her pride later, if He had time."

Abby walked over to the mirrored wall and rested her palm on it. The glass was smudged from years of fingertips—students checking posture, smoothing hair, pulling shoulders back like confidence was something you could adjust with enough effort.

"We were sought out," Abby said, voice softening. "We were booked. We were full. And then the lease said, 'Not anymore.'"

Anne stepped beside her. "It didn't say not anymore. It said pay more."

Ana lifted her basket. "And we said no."

Ada's eyes stayed on the mirror. "We said no to being bled slowly."

Amy's gaze drifted to the windows, to the street, to the city. "Manhattan can be beautiful, but it sure does charge for breathing."

Abby turned back to the group. "Now listen. Before anybody gets dramatic—"

"Too late," Amy said, holding up her tin. "I already ate a feeling."

Abby pointed at her. "You can eat your feelings when we get on the train. Right now we have business. We are not splitting up."

"Amen," Ana said instantly.

Anne nodded. "Agreed."

Ada said, "We decided."

Asha said, "We prayed."

Amy said, "And we promised."

Abby clapped once, sharp. "Good. Because we have families—mamas and daddies and siblings—but y'all are my family. And I am not about to go back to anybody's house like some sad little bird that fell out the nest."

Ana's eyes narrowed. "Especially not after we tasted freedom."

Anne slid the ledger into a satchel. "Freedom and responsibility. We did both."

Amy lifted her hand like she was in class. "Question."

Abby pointed. "Speak."

Amy cleared her throat. "Where exactly are we going?"

Silence fell again for half a second.

Then Anne said, "West."

Ana said, "Where rent doesn't try to eat your soul."

Asha said, "Where the Lord is already waiting."

Ada said, "Where we can build."

Abby said, "Where people don't act like a woman smiling is a public emergency."

Amy blinked. "That is not a map."

Anne reached into her satchel and pulled out a folded paper. "It is a map enough. I have researched. There is a rail line. There is a town. There is farmland."

Ana leaned in, eyes wide. "Town name?"

Anne spoke it like it mattered.

"Stillwater Crossing, Missouri."

Abby rolled the words around her mouth. "Stillwater. Crossing."

Ada nodded slowly. "A crossing is a decision."

Asha murmured, "And still water runs deep."

Amy clapped quietly. "It sounds like a place where a woman can breathe without apologizing."

Ana lifted her basket in victory. "It also sounds like a place hungry. And I have opinions about hunger."

Abby grinned. "Good. Because we are not going empty-handed. We are going with skills."

"And the Bible," Amy added.

"And prayer," Asha added.

"And common sense," Anne added.

"And dignity," Ada added.

"And bread," Ana added.

Abby stared at Ana. "Is bread your whole personality?"

Ana placed a hand over her heart. "No. Sometimes it's tamales."

Amy leaned back, laughing. "Lord, we are going to start a whole town by feeding it."

Anne gave Amy a look. "We are not starting a town."

Abby said, "We might improve one."

Ada's voice, low and sure: "We will."

The front door opened and a chilly gust came in, carrying street noise, horse hooves, and the smell of coal and winter.

A man stood there with a stiff posture and a polite face—polite in the way that meant he wanted to control the conversation before it started.

"Good morning," he said. "Misses... Stage?"

Six sets of eyes turned toward him.

Amy whispered, "Which one?"

He adjusted his hat and cleared his throat. "I— I am here from the property office. To confirm you have vacated."

Anne's eyebrows lifted. "We are in the act."

He looked past them at the mirror, the barre, the racks. "It's a shame. My wife—she attended once."

Abby smiled kindly. "Which class?"

"The waltz," he said quickly, then added, "She said you all were... lively."

Ana smiled wider. "We are alive, sir. It's a habit."

He blinked, uncertain what to do with that.

Ada stepped forward, her tone calm and unmovable. "We will leave the space clean."

"Yes," he said, relieved. "That's all. Just... a form."

Anne held out her hand. "Give it here."

He handed it to her, then hesitated. "Where will you go?"

Abby opened her mouth.

Anne spoke first. "West."

He seemed offended by the simplicity.

Ana tilted her head. "Did you think we were going to dissolve into mist because a lease ended?"

Amy's shoulders shook with quiet laughter.

Asha said softly, to no one in particular, "People often mistake paperwork for power."

The man's ears reddened. "I—well—good day."

He backed out and closed the door as if the room might chase him.

Abby exhaled. "He looked like he'd never seen six women stand still in their own decision."

Ada returned to the clothing rack, lifted a neatly folded garment bag, and said, "He has now."

Amy slid off the bench. "Alright. If we're leaving, then we need to do one last thing."

Anne frowned. "What?"

Amy walked to the center of the floor, placed her sweets tin down carefully, and held out her hands. "We pray."

Ana nodded immediately. "Yes."

Asha stepped closer, quiet and ready.

Ada's posture softened a fraction.

Abby said, "Right here on these boards."

Anne hesitated only a moment, then came in.

They formed a small circle in the middle of the studio, hands linked, palms warm, laughter lingering like perfume.

Amy began, voice gentle. "Jesus... thank You for seven years of work that was honest."

Ana added, "Thank You for customers who came proud and left smiling—sometimes confused, but smiling."

Abby said, "Thank You for feet that can still move and backs that can still straighten. Thank You for freedom."

Asha spoke softly, steady. "Thank You for guiding us by peace and not by fear."

Ada's voice came next—quiet, weighty. "Thank You for making us family. Keep us in love. Keep us in truth."

Anne finally said, "And give us exactly enough money. Again."

Amy let out a small laugh through the prayer. "Yes, Lord. Exactly enough."

They lifted their heads.

The room still looked like an ending.

But the air felt like a beginning.

Abby picked up her dance shoes and tied them to the outside of her trunk. "Alright, sisters."

Ana lifted her basket. "We leave today."

Anne tucked the form into her satchel. "Tickets are purchased."

Asha tied the last twine knot. "Peace is present."

Ada picked up the garment bags. "Dignity stays."

Amy grabbed the tin of sweets. "And joy is coming too."

Abby opened the door.

And Manhattan—loud, costly, dazzling Manhattan—met them like it always did.

But this time, the six women did not shrink.

They stepped out together, and none of them apologized.

They gathered up their belongings; luggage upon luggage.

By the time the sun climbed high enough to make Manhattan honest, the hallway outside the studio looked like a traveling wardrobe had exploded and politely decided to stay.

Trunks stood upright like sentries. Hat boxes were stacked three high. Carpetbags bulged with shoes that had known applause. Parasols leaned against the wall like they were eavesdropping. There were ribbons, shawls, gloves, scarves, extra skirts, backup skirts, emergency skirts, and one entire case labeled in Anne's neat handwriting:

NOT OPTIONAL.

Abby Stage stood in the middle of it all, hands planted on her hips, surveying the scene with the satisfied expression of a woman who believed deeply in preparation.

"Well," she said, nodding once, "we look like a parade."

Ana Stage adjusted her hat—wide-brimmed, feathered, and entirely unapologetic. "A respectable parade," she said. "One that smells like bread."

Amy Stage was perched on the edge of a trunk, tying the ribbons on her boots. Her dress hem hovered daringly above the ankle line, as if it had made a personal decision about freedom.

"If anyone faints," Amy said cheerfully, "it will not be my fault. Ankles were created by God."

Anne Stage raised an eyebrow. "So were boundaries."

"Yes," Amy said, standing and smoothing her skirt. "And sometimes God moves them."

Ada Stage said nothing. She simply adjusted her gloves—cream-colored, fitted, flawless— and checked the seam of her traveling dress. Her hem, too, rested just above what polite society preferred. She did not defend it. She did not explain it. She carried it.

Asha Stage lifted a small satchel and tucked it inside her larger bag. Inside were dried herbs, Scripture slips written in careful ink, and a worn Bible wrapped in cloth.

"They are heavy," Asha said softly, smiling to herself. "But not burdensome."

Abby grinned. "Speak for yourself. This trunk could sanctify a sinner if it fell on him."

It took three taxis.

Three patient drivers.

And one deeply confused doorman.

The women loaded luggage like professionals—efficient, practiced, laughing as if they had done this exact thing a hundred times before. Dresses swayed. Hats tilted. Ankles flashed. The city stared.

One man actually stopped walking.

Ana noticed. "Sir," she called kindly, "we are just leaving. You will survive."

The man blinked and removed his hat.

Amy leaned into Abby and whispered, "That's the power of coordinated confidence."

By the time they reached the rail station, hours had passed. The station itself breathed noise—porters calling, engines hissing, boots scuffing stone, voices echoing up into iron rafters like prayers that hadn't decided what they were yet.

They did not rush.

They moved together.

Abby tested a step on the polished floor and suddenly pivoted, skirts flaring just enough to cause a ripple of attention.

"Oh no," Anne warned. "Do not start."

"I am not starting," Abby said solemnly. "I am stretching."

Amy clapped once. "If we don't move, we'll stiffen."

Ana laughed. "Five counts. That's all."

And right there—between ticket counters and the luggage scale—the six women took five precise, compact steps. A half-turn. A pause. A gentle stomp.

Asha closed her eyes briefly. "The Lord is amused."

A porter stopped mid-step. "What... what was that?"

Abby smiled warmly. "Maintenance."

They purchased their tickets without hesitation.

First class.

Private car.

Anne counted twice before handing over the money.

"Worth it," she said firmly. "We are dancers."

"And loud," Amy added.

"And prayerful," Ana said.

"And hungry," Abby said.

They boarded their car at last—a polished, comfortable space with cushioned seats, curtained windows, and enough room to breathe. The door closed behind them with a satisfying finality.

Silence lasted exactly three seconds.

Then Amy laughed.

Then Abby kicked her heel lightly against the floor.

Then Ana clapped once, loud and joyful.

"We did it," she said. "We left."

Asha set her bag down and rested her hand on the window. "We obeyed peace."

Ada took a seat, smoothing her skirt. "We chose forward."

Anne dropped into a chair and exhaled. "We paid cash."

They stacked their luggage neatly, as if even their belongings understood discipline. Then Anne opened her satchel and pulled out a small stack of envelopes.

"Alright," she said. "Let us be adults."

Abby groaned. "You always say that right before math."

Anne ignored her and laid the envelopes out on the table. "Count with me."

They counted carefully.

Once.

Twice.

Then again, because Anne insisted.

Amy's eyes widened. "Five thousand dollars."

Ana crossed herself instinctively, then laughed. "Lord, You are generous."

Asha whispered, "Psalm thirty-seven, verse three: *Trust in the Lord and do good; dwell in the land and cultivate faithfulness.*"

Abby leaned back in her seat. "Well, we can definitely dwell."

Anne nodded. "And build."

She pulled out a folded paper—maps, notes, underlined phrases. "Stillwater Crossing has land near town. Homesteads available. Close enough to commerce. Far enough for quiet."

Ada leaned in. "Enough for a house?"

"Yes," Anne said. "And possibly one or two storefronts."

Amy gasped. "And the studio?"

Anne smiled, thin and satisfied. "Especially the studio."

Ana pressed her hands together. "Lord, You are showing off."

The train jolted gently, then began to move.

The city slid past the windows, brick and iron giving way to wider skies.

Abby stood. "Before we get too settled—"

Amy interrupted, "We pray again."

Abby smiled. "Exactly."

They gathered, some sitting, some standing, hands linked awkwardly around the small table.

Ana prayed aloud, voice rich and sure. "Jesus, we thank You for leading us not by fear, not by lack, but by promise."

Amy added, "We thank You that You delight in life, and that You made joy on purpose."

Asha spoke softly. "Your word says in Proverbs sixteen, verse three: *Commit your works to the Lord and your plans will be established.* We are committing."

Ada's voice followed, steady. "Teach us to love as You commanded—*'You are My friends if you do what I command,'* just as You said in John fifteen, fourteen."

Anne concluded, practical and reverent. "And help us steward every dollar like it already belongs to You."

They opened their Bibles afterward, reading aloud, passing verses back and forth like shared bread.

Amy read Psalm one twenty-seven and laughed softly. "*Unless the Lord builds the house...* Well. That settles that."

Abby read Hebrews twelve and tapped the page. "*Run with endurance.* Dancers understand that."

Ana read Matthew six and shook her head. "*Do not worry about tomorrow.* I am trying."

Asha simply listened, eyes closed, peace resting on her like a shawl.

As the hours passed, they grew louder.

Not unruly—joyful.

They discussed floor plans. Recipes. Fabric costs. How much flour it would take to feed a town that didn't know it was hungry yet.

They practiced a new step in the narrow aisle, careful not to knock lamps loose.

Abby whispered, "Three counts only."

Amy whispered back, "Four is better."

Ana laughed. "Five. For grace."

The train rocked gently as they moved, skirts brushing, laughter lifting.

A man passed by the door, paused, and then kept walking, smiling to himself.

Anne watched him go. "We are going to be talked about."

Ada said calmly, "We already are."

Night settled in.

Lamplight warmed the car.

They sat together, tired and content, heads leaning, Scripture open, future unfolding.

Abby whispered, almost to herself, "The studio closed."

Ana smiled. "But the calling didn't."

Asha murmured, "The Lord goes with us."

And as the train carried them westward—loud, prayerful, dancing even in stillness—He did.

Chapter Two

The train schedule with all the stops was going to take two weeks.

That fact alone would have troubled sensible people.

The six Stage women, however, treated it like an invitation.

Two weeks meant pauses. Two weeks meant watching towns instead of rushing past them. Two weeks meant room for prayer, laughter, meals that lasted longer than manners expected, and the freedom to stretch legs that had spent years obeying narrow stages and narrower opinions.

The conductor explained it plainly when Anne asked.

"We stop often," he said. "Freight. Passengers. Livestock. Mail. Some towns you'll stay half a day. Some overnight."

Anne nodded, calculating. "And sleeping arrangements?"

"You're free to board in town if you wish," he said.

Abby smiled sweetly. "We won't."

He blinked. "Ma'am?"

"We sleep on the train," Abby said again, as if that settled the matter of the world.

And it did.

Every town they passed through offered boardinghouses—some clean, some curious, some openly judgmental the moment six women stepped down in hats, color, movement, and hems that defied expectation. But the Stage women always returned to their private car when evening came, laughing and tired, skirts dusty, hands full of parcels and stories.

"This car is ours," Amy declared the first night, kicking off her boots and sighing with satisfaction. "It doesn't whisper when we walk."

Ana nodded. "And it doesn't ask what church we belong to before offering a pillow."

Asha smiled gently. "It lets us rest."

They had paid for first class, and they used it without apology.

The food arrived on white plates with silver edges. Hot bread. Butter that melted on contact. Stews that had actually seen seasoning. Coffee strong enough to wake repentance.

Amy nearly cried the first morning.

"I forgot food could love you back," she said, dabbing her mouth.

Anne raised a brow. "Remember this when you budget."

"This is not budget food," Amy said solemnly. "This is provision."

They entered the first-class dining car together, every time. Not because they were making a statement—though one was made—but because they were not going to split themselves into smaller pieces for anyone's comfort.

The stares came.

Some were curious. Some appreciative. Some tight-lipped and offended.

Christian men frowned first, usually after glancing at the ankles. Christian women frowned longer, their eyes moving from hem to hat to posture and back again, as if searching for permission to disapprove.

One woman whispered loudly enough to be sure she was heard, "They must be performers."

Abby leaned toward Amy. "We are."

Amy whispered back, "And they are."

Ana laughed into her napkin.

Men, on the other hand, tried a different tactic.

They leaned in.

They smiled sideways.

They waited until the women were seated before asking questions that pretended to be polite.

"Traveling alone?" one man asked.

Anne answered without looking up from her plate. "Together."

Another tried, "Must be lonely, without husbands."

Abby smiled kindly. "Sir, you don't know us nearly well enough to say that."

A third attempted a whisper when the others stood to leave. "Perhaps we could speak privately?"

Amy laughed outright. "Oh no, thank you. We prefer daylight."

They knew the game.

They had grown up in it.

New York City taught you early how to hear what wasn't said and refuse it without flinching.

The money they spent on food and comfort did not trouble them. It was not part of the five thousand they had counted and prayed over. That sum was sacred. Set apart. Purpose-bound.

The train money came from tips.

From coins tossed on stages after a particularly daring turn.

From folded bills slipped into baskets after performances that stirred something unnamed.

From applause translated into currency.

"This," Abby said once, holding up a handful of coins before handing them to the steward, "is the sound of joy."

They ate what they wanted.

They talked how they wanted.

Sometimes louder than expected.

Sometimes softer than suspicion allowed.

They prayed before meals—not quietly, not performatively, but naturally.

"Father, thank You for feeding us," Ana would say, voice warm and clear. "Thank You for strength and mercy and good digestion."

Heads would turn.

Amy once added cheerfully, "And thank You for butter."

Asha would smile and whisper a verse afterward, "The Lord is my shepherd; I shall not want."

Sometimes they sang under their breath.

Sometimes they laughed mid-prayer because Abby tripped over a chair.

Once, they danced into the dining car.

It was not planned.

It simply happened.

The train had stopped longer than expected. The air felt restless. Abby stood first, stretching.

"I need to move," she said.

Amy was already on her feet. "Me too."

Ana clapped once. "Just a little."

Anne sighed. "No one knock anything over."

Asha nodded. "Keep it contained."

Contained lasted four counts.

They moved between tables with careful grace—skirts lifted just enough to clear feet, steps light, rhythm alive. It was not a performance so much as a reminder that bodies were meant to do more than sit still and be judged.

A child clapped.

An old woman smiled.

One man looked scandalized.

Another looked like he had remembered something important and forgotten it again.

When they finished, Abby bowed slightly. "Thank you for your patience."

The steward stared, then laughed. "Well," he said, "that's a first."

The towns blurred together—names announced, platforms crowded, goods loaded, lives intersecting briefly before moving on.

They stepped down often.

They observed.

They listened.

They prayed quietly in alleys and loudly in fields.

They always returned to the train to sleep.

"This bed," Amy said one night, sighing, "has seen more honesty than most parlors."

Anne adjusted the curtain. "It costs extra."

"Yes," Amy said. "And it's worth every cent."

They read Scripture together each night, lamps glowing low.

Sometimes one verse.

Sometimes whole chapters.

John fifteen became a favorite.

"'Love one another as I have loved you,'" Ana read once, closing the book afterward. "That is enough religion for me."

Abby nodded. "It takes courage, though."

Asha said softly, "And surrender."

Anne added, "And wisdom."

Amy smiled. "And joy."

Outside, the train kept moving—slow, deliberate, unashamed of its pace.

Inside, six women laughed, prayed, ate, danced, and trusted.

Two weeks was not a delay.

It was preparation.

And Stillwater Crossing waited, whether it knew it yet or not.

Chapter Three

The Harvey Farm—and the Woman Who Was Not There

The Harvey Farm lay just beyond the town limits of Stillwater Crossing, Missouri, where the land opened itself wide and honest, as if nothing had ever needed to be hidden there. The soil was dark and willing. The fences were straight. The barns stood red and dependable against the horizon. Every gate closed the way it was meant to. Every path had been walked so many times it remembered the weight of boots.

It was a farm built on order.

Six sons had grown up on that land, their lives shaped by its rhythms—sunrise work, measured meals, Scripture read clean and clear at the table, prayer offered with heads bowed and backs straight. The farm prospered quietly, as if it approved of restraint.

That fact was spoken of with gratitude and gravity.

Herbert Harvey was sixty-five years old—tall, broad, unbent by time. His hands were large and steady, marked by work rather than age. His shoulders still carried authority naturally, without announcement. He was a man who believed God honored discipline, order, and restraint, and his life seemed to confirm it.

Six sons raised.
Land prospering.
No scandals.
No visible rebellion.

He gave thanks daily.

And yet, the house had been quieter than it needed to be for years.

Because Herbert Harvey's wife was not dead.

She was simply not home.

Her name was **Hannah Harvey**—and that name was now locked into the marrow of this story.

Hannah Harvey was sixty years old, tall as many men, standing just shy of six feet, her posture elegant without effort. Time had been kind to her in the way that mattered—her figure full and generous, her movements still graceful even when slowed by years. Her skin carried a golden warmth, her long black hair fell in soft waves when unbound, and her laughter—though quieter than it once had been—still knew where it came from.

Hannah had been a dancer.

A real one.

Before Missouri.
Before the farm.
Before stillness learned to masquerade as holiness.

She had loved twirling, spinning skirts, quick turns that lifted the heart and loosened the soul. Dancing had once been prayer for her— movement offered up in joy.

But the church had frowned.

And her husband, though loving, had agreed with the church.

Marriage, he believed, required leaving some things behind.

So Hannah had.

The dancing stopped.

The laughter softened.

The twirls became memories she revisited only in private, sometimes in dreams where her body remembered what her waking life no longer allowed.

She had met Herbert in Baltimore.

He had been there for a cattle ranch association meeting—formal, rigid, uncomfortable in city spaces that smelled like perfume and ambition. She had been a waiter at a high-end hotel, moving through the room with natural grace, her presence impossible to ignore even when she tried.

He had asked to speak with her after her shift.

She had smiled and said yes—only if her mother was present.

He had laughed, genuinely, and agreed.

They had spoken with her mother seated nearby, eyes sharp and approving. They had spoken again. And again.

Before Herbert returned west, they had married.

It had been fast.

And true.

They loved Jesus.

They loved each other.

Hannah had left the city behind.

She had cooked for Herbert and their sons with devotion—Mexican dishes rich with history, recipes taught by her mother and sisters. She had six sisters, all beautiful, all strong, all devoted to family. They rotated care for their aging parents, and every three years Hannah returned east for six months at a time.

This time, she was coming home.

She had boarded the train in first class, choosing a longer route—fourteen days instead of the shortest passage—because something in her wanted to see the West again slowly. To feel the land change. To remember herself before she stepped back into routine.

Three days into the journey, she noticed them.

Six women.

They were impossible not to notice.

They moved together even when seated. Their laughter rose freely. Their prayers were spoken naturally, without self-consciousness. Their dresses defied polite ankle expectations, their hats bold, their presence alive.

Hannah watched them over her teacup, curiosity stirring something long quiet.

"They are dancers," she murmured.

She knew movement when she saw it.

They were roughly the same ages as her sons.

That unsettled her.

Not unpleasantly.

But profoundly.

She watched them speak Scripture as conversation. She watched them eat without shame. She watched them laugh without apology.

And she wondered where they were going.

And why.

Across the car, the women noticed her.

Abby leaned in first. "Who is she?"

Ada followed her gaze. "She carries herself like someone who has lived."

Amy's eyes widened. "And like someone who remembers how to dance."

Ana smiled softly. "She looks kind."

Asha said quietly, "She is holding longing."

Hannah felt their attention and met it easily.

She smiled.

The smile crossed the space like permission.

Abby stood.

"Ma'am," she said warmly, "we hope we aren't being disruptive."

Hannah laughed—a soft, surprised sound. "You are not disruptive. You are refreshing."

Amy blinked. "That is the nicest thing anyone has said to us all week."

Hannah gestured to the empty seat beside her. "Please. Sit. I would like to know who you are."

They gathered, skirts brushing, laughter still humming beneath their movements.

"My name is Hannah Harvey," she said. "I am on my way home."

Abby answered without hesitation. "Then we are glad to meet you on the way."

Ana added, "We are traveling west too."

Hannah studied them. "Together?"

"Always," Amy said.

Asha nodded. "We are family."

Hannah's chest tightened unexpectedly.

"And what do you call yourselves?" she asked.

Abby glanced around at the others, then smiled.

"We are **The Stage Sisters**," she said.

The name settled into place as if it had always been waiting.

Hannah repeated it softly. "The Stage Sisters."

"Yes, ma'am," Amy said. "Six of us. Seven years together."

Hannah's eyes warmed. "I was a dancer once."

Silence fell—not awkward, but reverent.

Abby spoke carefully. "Once?"

Hannah smiled, wistful but unashamed. "A long time ago."

Ana reached for her hand without thinking. "Then you never stopped."

Hannah laughed, and for just a moment, she imagined herself twirling again.

Outside, the train rolled westward.

Inside, past and future leaned toward one another.

And far away, the Harvey Farm waited— unaware that its stillness was about to be tested by joy.

The stage sisters talk about themselves and where they are going and to Hannah's amazement to her hometown.

Hannah Harvey listened the way a woman listens when something familiar begins to stir after years of quiet. Not with interruption. Not with suspicion. But with a patience shaped by memory.

"The Stage Sisters," she repeated again, as if tasting the name to see whether it held weight.

Abby nodded. "We didn't name ourselves at first. Other people did. We just stopped correcting them."

Amy laughed. "It was either that or 'those women who won't sit down.'"

Ana leaned forward, elbows on knees, eyes bright. "We taught dance. All kinds. Waltzes for the careful. Folk steps for the brave. Some things we made up when the music demanded it."

Asha added softly, "Movement has language. People hear what they are ready for."

Hannah smiled at that, slow and thoughtful. "Yes. That's true."

She studied them more closely now—their posture, the way their hands moved even while speaking, the way their laughter came easily but did not feel careless. These were women who had worked, prayed, failed, tried again, and kept choosing one another.

"And where are you going?" Hannah asked at last.

The question hung in the air for half a breath.

Anne answered first, precise as always. "Missouri."

Hannah's fingers stilled around her teacup.

"Missouri," she echoed.

Abby grinned. "Stillwater Crossing, to be exact."

For a moment, the steady rhythm of the train seemed to change, as if it had noticed too.

Hannah's breath caught—not dramatically, not visibly, but enough that she had to set her cup down.

"That," she said slowly, "is my home."

Six faces turned toward her at once.

Amy blinked. "Your home-home?"

"Yes," Hannah said, voice calm though her heart had begun to move faster. "My husband's farm is just outside town."

Ana laughed softly, astonished. "Jesus does like to surprise people."

Abby sat back, eyes wide. "Well. That explains why you felt... familiar."

Hannah smiled, a little shaken now. "And why you felt like something I had been waiting for without knowing."

Anne recovered first. "Stillwater Crossing is small."

"Yes," Hannah said. "Orderly. Quiet."

Abby tilted her head. "Restrained?"

Hannah laughed under her breath. "That is a polite word for it."

Amy leaned closer. "Do they like dancing?"

Hannah hesitated.

That hesitation told them everything.

"They prefer stillness," Hannah said carefully. "And propriety."

Ana nodded. "We are going to be talked about."

"Yes," Hannah agreed. "You will."

Abby smiled. "Good. We were worried we'd be bored."

Hannah laughed then—really laughed—and the sound startled her. It rose from somewhere deep, unpracticed, almost forgotten.

"You are not what Stillwater Crossing expects," she said.

Amy shrugged. "We rarely are."

Asha spoke gently. "Expectation is not the same as calling."

Hannah looked at her with new interest. "You pray like someone who listens."

Asha inclined her head. "I learned to."

Silence settled—not heavy, but full.

Hannah broke it. "Tell me about the seven years."

Abby didn't hesitate. "We survived New York."

"That is a testimony," Hannah said sincerely.

Amy laughed. "We taught society ladies to breathe."

Ana added, "And to eat."

Anne said, "And to balance accounts."

Ada said quietly, "And to stand upright."

They took turns then, voices overlapping, stories weaving—of late nights and early mornings, of students who cried when they learned they could move without shame, of money scraped together and prayers whispered over rent notices.

Hannah listened, her hands folded in her lap, eyes bright with recognition.

"You loved one another," she said finally.

"Yes," Abby said simply. "We still do."

Hannah swallowed. "That kind of love... it costs something."

Anne nodded. "Everything worth having does."

The train slowed briefly, then resumed its pace.

Outside, the land was changing—buildings thinning, horizons widening.

Hannah felt as if she were crossing something unseen.

"My husband," she said after a moment, "is a good man."

They waited.

"He believes deeply in order," she continued. "In restraint. In the kind of righteousness that looks tidy."

Abby smiled gently. "Those men exist."

Hannah's eyes softened. "He does not know what to do with joy that moves."

Amy tilted her head. "That can be taught."

Hannah shook her head. "Or resisted."

Ana reached across the small table and took Hannah's hand, warm and steady. "Sometimes God sends joy anyway."

Hannah's fingers tightened slightly. "Sometimes He does."

She thought of the farm—of Herbert standing straight at the table, of six sons grown into men who worked hard and spoke carefully, of a house that functioned well and laughed rarely.

She thought of the mother who had died giving birth to the youngest, of the silence that had settled like a rule afterward.

She thought of herself, dreaming of movement.

"And you?" Abby asked gently. "Why did you take the long route home?"

Hannah considered lying.

Instead, she told the truth.

"Because I wanted to remember who I was before I learned to be quiet," she said.

No one spoke for a moment.

Then Amy smiled. "You picked the right train."

Asha added, "And the right company."

The steward passed by and glanced in, smiling at the sight of them gathered, voices low and warm.

"Everything alright, ladies?"

"Yes," Hannah said, surprising herself by answering. "Everything is."

As evening deepened, lamps were lit again. Scripture was read aloud—not formally, but shared. Psalm 68 was quoted. John 15 returned, as it often did.

"I have called you friends," Amy read, her voice soft.

Hannah closed her eyes.

Friends.

She had been a wife. A mother. A caretaker. A woman of faith.

But friendship—this kind—had been absent longer than she realized.

"You know," Hannah said quietly, "my sons are your age."

Abby smiled. "That tracks."

Hannah raised a brow. "How so?"

"You look like a woman who raised men," Abby said. "Strong ones."

Hannah's pride was immediate and unashamed. "They are handsome. Hardworking. Devout."

Ana grinned. "And unmarried?"

Hannah sighed. "Yes."

Amy clasped her hands dramatically. "Well. That is interesting."

Anne shot her a look. "Do not."

"I am only observing," Amy said innocently.

Hannah laughed again, the sound freer now. "They claim the farm needs them."

Abby nodded thoughtfully. "It often does— until it doesn't."

The train whistle sounded in the distance, long and low.

Somewhere ahead lay Stillwater Crossing.

Hannah looked at the six women—these Stage Sisters who moved like prayer and laughed like grace—and wondered what would happen when they stepped onto Missouri soil.

She wondered what would happen to her.

Outside, the land waited.

Inside, something long restrained had begun to breathe.

Chapter Four

Stops, Steps, and a Grand Intention

By the time the train reached its fourth long stop, Hannah Harvey no longer felt like a passenger.

She felt like she had been reclaimed.

The train had slowed into towns that smelled of coal, bread, horses, and expectation. Sometimes it stayed only an hour. Sometimes three. Once, nearly half a day. And every time the wheels stilled long enough for the body to remember itself, the Stage Sisters gathered Hannah up like a secret they had decided to keep.

"Shoes off," Abby said the first time, already tugging at her own boots.

Hannah blinked. "Outside?"

"Yes," Amy said brightly. "The earth likes feet."

Anne glanced around. "We are not breaking laws. Just expectations."

Ana laughed. "Those are already broken."

They stepped down from the train platform into open space—packed dirt, wooden planks, sometimes grass brave enough to grow near rail lines. Curious eyes followed. Disapproving ones too.

Hannah hesitated only once.

Then Abby took her hands.

"Trust us," she said. "Your body remembers."

And it did.

The first step was small. Careful. Almost shy.

The second came easier.

By the third, Hannah was laughing.

Not the polite laugh she had practiced for years. The real one. The one that startled her with its volume and loosened something in her chest she hadn't realized was clenched.

"Again," she said breathlessly. "Do that again."

Amy clapped. "She's back!"

Asha smiled, watching closely. "She never left."

They taught her new steps—quick turns, grounded footwork, movements that didn't ask permission from the waist up or apologize below the ankle.

And Hannah taught them too.

Steps she had learned as a girl. Turns passed down through family gatherings. Movements meant for laughter more than performance. For circles, not lines.

Ana gasped at one of them. "That is beautiful."

Hannah grinned. "That one is older than my mother."

Abby wiped sweat from her brow. "I like old things."

People stared.

Some smiled.

Some frowned deeply, as if witnessing something improper and contagious.

One man muttered, "That's not decent."

Amy smiled sweetly. "Neither is judgment, but here we are."

Hannah danced anyway.

She danced with her long black hair loose, her skirts lifted just enough to move freely, her posture proud and unafraid. She danced with the grace of a woman who had been waiting twenty years for permission she no longer needed.

"This," she said one afternoon, breathless and glowing, "is the best I have felt since my wedding."

Abby raised a brow. "Careful."

Hannah laughed. "Since the honeymoon, then."

They protected her.

Naturally.

When looks lingered too long, Abby stepped closer. When whispers sharpened, Anne's gaze cooled the air. When someone scoffed openly, Ana offered bread with such warmth it left no room for offense.

And Asha prayed.

Quietly. Constantly.

Hannah noticed.

"You pray without making it heavy," she said once.

Asha smiled. "God is not heavy."

As the days passed, Hannah stopped worrying about who might object.

Because joy had returned to her body, and she had no intention of surrendering it again.

Stillwater Crossing crept closer with each mile.

And with it, Hannah's thoughts sharpened.

One afternoon, while the Stage Sisters were debating whether a particular turn counted as a spin or a leap, Hannah slipped away.

Just briefly.

She stepped into the telegraph office of a tidy little town whose name she barely noticed. She wrote carefully, firmly, and with satisfaction.

HERBERT HARVEY STOP
ARRIVING STILLWATER CROSSING
EXACT DATE FOUR DAYS STOP
ALL SONS PRESENT STOP
CLEAN SHAVEN AND HAIR CUT STOP
HOUSE CLEANED THOROUGHLY
STOP
WAGONS FOR LUGGAGE STOP
PREPARE GRAND MEAL STOP
THIS IS NOT A REQUEST STOP
LOVE HANNAH

She handed it over with a smile.

The clerk blinked. "Ma'am?"

"Yes?"

"That's... very specific."

Hannah smiled wider. "It needs to be."

She returned to the train as if nothing at all had happened.

The Stage Sisters noticed immediately.

"You look pleased," Amy said.

Hannah folded her hands in her lap. "I am."

Abby narrowed her eyes playfully. "You did something."

"Possibly," Hannah said serenely.

Ana laughed. "Oh, I like her."

As the sun dipped low that evening, Hannah watched the women dance again, her heart full and busy.

She imagined Stillwater Crossing.

The farm.

Herbert standing stiffly at first, then softening.

Her sons—tall, strong, orderly—clean-shaven and bewildered.

She imagined introductions.

Conversations.

Laughter where there had been silence.

She imagined grandchildren with curls and color and music in their feet. Children who danced as easily as they prayed. A family that looked like heaven had decided to be creative.

She smiled to herself.

The Stage Sisters had no idea.

Not yet.

They laughed and danced and teased one another, unaware that Hannah Harvey had already begun arranging the future.

The train rolled on.

And Stillwater Crossing was about to receive more than it expected.

Questions, Land, and the Kind of Trouble That Builds Things

The sun dipped low enough to soften the edges of the world, turning the rail platform gold and forgiving. The train had stopped again—another long pause, another town with a name that would soon blur into memory. Crates were loaded. Barrels rolled. Voices rose and fell like waves.

The Stage Sisters had settled Hannah comfortably on a bench near the edge of the train platform, skirts spread, shoes kicked off, hair loosened by joy and motion.

Amy fanned herself with her hat. "Alright, Hannah Harvey. Since you have clearly decided to adopt us—"

"I have not adopted anyone," Hannah said calmly.

"—we have questions," Amy finished, ignoring her.

Abby nodded. "Important ones."

Anne leaned forward, business already sharpening her tone. "Tell us about Stillwater Crossing."

Hannah smiled into her teacup. "What would you like to know?"

Ana didn't hesitate. "Land."

Of course.

"How much," Anne added, "and how close."

Hannah considered them carefully. She had lived long enough to know when women were not speaking hypothetically.

"Well," she began, "there is land in town— small parcels, close to Main Street. Not many, but some. Shops, old buildings that haven't been used properly in years."

Amy's eyes lit. "Unused space is a cry for redemption."

Anne nodded approvingly. "And outside of town?"

"Plenty," Hannah said. "Large parcels. Good soil. Some already cleared. Some waiting for purpose."

Abby stretched her legs. "Could a person build both?"

"Yes," Hannah said. "If a person had vision. And stamina."

Ana clasped her hands. "And permission."

Hannah tilted her head. "Stillwater Crossing respects ownership. Less so ambition."

Amy laughed. "Oh, we will be discussed."

"That is guaranteed," Hannah agreed.

They fell quiet for a moment, the wheels of imagination turning louder than the train.

Asha spoke next, her voice gentle but firm. "We want to build things that heal."

Hannah looked at her. "Such as?"

"A place for women," Asha said. "Especially those who want to leave certain lives behind."

Abby nodded. "Soiled doves."

Hannah did not flinch.

"Yes," Hannah said. "The saloons."

Ana leaned forward, eyes earnest. "We don't want to save them. We want to give them work. Bread. Skill."

Amy added, "And joy."

Anne said, "And income."

Abby finished, "And dignity."

Hannah let out a slow breath. "That will unsettle people."

Amy smiled. "We specialize in that."

66

Hannah laughed quietly. "Stillwater Crossing has rules. Unspoken ones."

Anne crossed her arms. "We have survived New York."

"That is different," Hannah said. "New York judges loudly. Stillwater judges silently."

Abby shrugged. "Silence is easier to interrupt."

They laughed.

Hannah watched them—really watched them now—and felt something shift again. These women were not reckless. They were deliberate. Their joy was not careless. It was chosen.

"Tell us the truth," Abby said gently. "Is there room for us?"

Hannah answered honestly. "There is room. But not readiness."

Ana smiled. "Good. Readiness rarely grows without friction."

The train whistle blew once—low and patient.

They stayed seated.

Amy leaned back. "What about baking? Bread sells everywhere."

"Yes," Hannah said. "The town buys flour and sugar from the mercantile. But there is no dedicated bakery."

Ana clapped once. "There will be."

Anne's pen was already moving. "Dressmaking?"

Hannah nodded. "Women order from catalogs. Fit is... inconsistent."

Ada, who had been listening quietly, spoke at last. "They deserve better."

"Yes," Hannah said softly. "They do."

"And dance," Abby added. "A proper hall."

Hannah hesitated—not because she doubted them, but because she understood the weight of that particular disruption.

"Dance," Hannah said slowly, "will be the hardest sell."

Amy grinned. "Then it is the most necessary."

Asha smiled. "Movement frees what words cannot."

Hannah studied her. "You speak like someone who has seen restraint wound people."

Asha nodded once. "Yes."

The platform had emptied. The sun leaned lower. Somewhere nearby, a woman watched them with curiosity. A man shook his head and walked away.

Hannah felt no urge to shrink.

"You should know," Hannah said carefully, "my sons are... disciplined."

Abby perked up. "How disciplined?"

"Very," Hannah said. "Order, routine, restraint."

Amy laughed. "Lord, they are going to need us."

Hannah smiled, but her eyes grew thoughtful. "They are good men."

"We believe you," Ana said warmly.

Hannah folded her hands. "They cook. All of them."

Amy gasped. "This is important information."

"And they work hard," Hannah continued. "They believe provision is love."

Anne nodded. "That belief can be expanded."

Hannah smiled knowingly. "That is what I am counting on."

Abby tilted her head. "You are planning something."

Hannah met her gaze evenly. "I am a mother."

That answer explained everything.

The train hissed, preparing to move again.

They gathered their shoes, their hats, their laughter.

As they climbed back aboard, Amy leaned close to Hannah. "You are enjoying this."

Hannah did not deny it. "I am."

Inside the car, the air felt warm and conspiratorial.

Anne spread out her notes. "If we purchase small parcels in town, we establish presence. If we purchase a larger parcel outside town, we build sustainability."

Abby nodded. "And a studio."

Ana added, "And kitchens."

Ada said, "And rooms where women are seen."

Asha said quietly, "And prayer."

Hannah listened, her heart full and busy.

She knew enough to keep them dreaming.

She knew the town's resistance. She knew its hunger. She knew the men who would object and the women who would secretly hope.

She knew her husband would stand tall and uncertain.

She knew her sons would be present, clean-shaven, prepared, and unprepared all at once.

She smiled to herself.

Stillwater Crossing thought it was waiting for a train.

It was not.

It was waiting for a reckoning wrapped in joy, flour-dusted hands, moving feet, and women who refused to apologize for bringing life with them.

The Stage Sisters talked late into the night, planning bakeries and sewing rooms and a dance hall where even broken stories could learn new steps.

Hannah listened.

And dreamed.

And did not warn them.

Because some surprises are holy.

Chapter Five

Two Days Before Stillwater

There were only two days left on the train.

That fact settled over the Stage Sisters like a soft bell—gentle, inevitable, impossible to ignore. The rhythm of the rails felt different now, as if even the iron knew it was nearing a conclusion and something else entirely.

Hannah Harvey sat by the window, hands folded, watching the land stretch wider with every mile. Her reflection stared back at her— tall, elegant, composed—and for the first time in years, she did not feel invisible inside her own skin.

Abby leaned against the opposite seat and studied her critically.

"Hannah," she said slowly, "when was the last time you let yourself be admired?"

Hannah laughed lightly. "I am admired."

Amy tilted her head. "By who?"

"My husband," Hannah said. "Occasionally. My sons, when they remember."

Ana smiled gently. "That is not the same thing."

Hannah raised a brow. "I beg your pardon?"

Abby grinned. "It is time."

"For what?" Hannah asked, though something in her chest already knew.

Amy clasped her hands. "For presentation."

Anne looked up from her notes. "Strategic presentation."

Asha smiled, serene. "Joyful presentation."

Hannah laughed again, louder this time. "Oh no. I recognize that look. What are you planning?"

Abby answered without hesitation. "We are making you beautiful for your husband."

Hannah froze.

Then she laughed so hard she had to grip the armrest.

"I am already beautiful," she said, breathless.

"Yes," Abby agreed. "But we intend to be excessive."

Amy bounced in her seat. "Trinkets."

Ana nodded enthusiastically. "A scarf."

Anne added, practical as ever, "Bangles. Tasteful ones."

Asha said softly, "And curls. More curls."

Hannah shook her head, smiling helplessly. "You are impossible."

Abby leaned forward. "Do you object?"

Hannah considered.

Twenty years of restraint whispered caution.

Then she remembered dancing on platforms. Laughing freely. Telegraphing demands to her household without apology.

"No," she said finally. "I do not object."

Amy clapped. "Excellent."

Abby grinned. "Do you agree to full participation?"

Hannah hesitated only a moment. "Yes."

Ana laughed. "Might as well stir things up in advance."

Hannah smiled mischievously. "That was my thought exactly."

They spent the afternoon like conspirators.

Scarves were brought out—silk and cotton, colors that caught the light and framed Hannah's face like celebration. Trinkets appeared from pockets and bags—small earrings, a delicate chain, bangles that chimed softly when she moved.

Amy held up a scarf. "This one."

Anne shook her head. "Too subtle."

Abby snatched another. "This one."

Asha nodded. "That one remembers sunlight."

They tied it loosely around Hannah's neck, letting it fall naturally.

Ana stepped back and sighed. "Your husband is about to forget his own name."

Hannah laughed, cheeks warm. "You are terrible influences."

"Yes," Abby said proudly. "And effective."

Then came the hair.

Amy and Asha worked together, coaxing Hannah's long black waves into fuller curls, lifting volume where years of habit had smoothed it away.

Hannah watched in the mirror, astonished.

"I had forgotten," she murmured, "that my hair does this."

Asha smiled. "Your body remembers joy."

Anne observed critically. "We are not done."

By evening, Hannah looked radiant—still dignified, still herself, but alive in a way that could not be mistaken.

Abby stepped back and nodded once. "Perfect."

Hannah met her own eyes in the glass and felt something unfamiliar.

Anticipation.

The plan was finalized over supper.

"Here is how it goes," Abby said, serious now. "When we arrive, you step off first."

Hannah raised an eyebrow. "Alone?"

"Yes," Amy said. "Let the family react."

Ana grinned. "Let them adjust."

Anne added, "Give them thirty seconds."

Abby continued, "Then we follow."

Amy's eyes sparkled. "Flamboyant."

"Colorful," Ana added.

"Ankle-high boots," Abby said firmly.

"And dresses," Amy chimed in.

"Feathered hats," Ana finished.

Hannah laughed, shaking her head. "You intend to cause a scene."

Abby smiled. "We intend to make an entrance."

Hannah did not object.

What Hannah did not know—what none of the Stage Sisters knew—was that Stillwater Crossing was already buzzing.

There was talk.

Men gathered in low voices at the mercantile. At the church steps. At the edge of fields.

A train was coming.

Not this one.

Another.

A bridal train.

It was scheduled to arrive in a few days.

Women—some refined, some raised carefully, some chosen by reputation—would be brought west to meet men seeking wives. The meetings would be supervised. Orderly. Respectable.

The women would choose.

Or decline.

If they chose no one, they could leave on the next scheduled train.

It was all very dignified.

The Harvey boys had heard about it.

They stood together in the barn one evening, discussing it with their father.

"Seems sensible," Sam said.

"Orderly," Seth agreed.

"A good way to ensure standards," Saul added.

Scott said nothing but listened carefully.

Shane, youngest, shifted uncomfortably. "It sounds... strange."

Herbert Harvey stood with arms crossed, thoughtful. "Marriage requires wisdom," he said. "And compatibility."

"And faith," Seth added.

"Yes," Herbert said. "Faith."

They imagined women who would fit neatly into their lives.

Women who would not disrupt the farm.

Women who would not draw attention.

Women who would not dance in train stations.

They spoke with confidence.

They did not know the train that would arrive first had already begun rearranging everything.

And two days away, six women laughed softly, adjusting scarves and planning an entrance that Stillwater Crossing would never forget.

Morning Before Arrival

Morning arrived before anyone was ready for it.

On the train, it came softly—light slipping through curtains, the steady hum of wheels slowing just enough to announce intention. Two days had disappeared quicker than expected, and now there was only one hour

left before the conductor would call out the
name that had been living in all of them like a
held breath.

Stillwater Crossing.

Hannah Harvey woke before the knock.

She lay still for a moment, hands folded over her middle, listening to the rhythm beneath her. The train felt different now—less wandering, more purposeful. She smiled into the quiet, already knowing what the day held.

Across the car, the Stage Sisters were not nearly as composed.

Abby was already upright, tying her boots with decisive tugs.
Amy was brushing curls and humming under her breath.
Ana was rearranging scarves like offerings on an altar.
Anne was checking bags and rechecking them.
Asha sat by the window, eyes closed, praying quietly without moving her lips.
Ada stood calmly, smoothing fabric, observing everything.

Amy whispered loudly, "One hour."

Abby nodded. "Plenty of time."

Anne snorted. "It is not."

Ana laughed. "Everything happens in God's time."

Anne looked up. "God also invented clocks."

Hannah sat up, amused. "You are all up early."

Amy grinned. "So are you."

"Yes," Hannah said. "I could not sleep. I felt... anticipated."

Abby's eyes softened. "That is because you are about to be received."

Hannah breathed that in. Received. Not inspected. Not evaluated. Received.

They finished dressing her carefully—nothing excessive, nothing restrained. The scarf lay perfectly. The bangles chimed softly when she moved. Her curls framed her face in living waves.

Hannah looked in the mirror once more and laughed quietly. "My husband is going to think I've been stolen."

Abby smiled. "Borrowed by joy."

Meanwhile, miles ahead and already awake, the **Harvey men** had risen long before the sun cleared the edge of the fields.

They did not complain.

They never did.

Honor was a habit in that house.

Sam was first, as always, splashing water on his face at the wash basin, scrubbing hard as if discipline could be rubbed in deeper. Seth followed, humming a hymn under his breath. Silas moved quietly, efficient and wordless. Saul inspected his boots with sharp attention. Scott lingered, thoughtful. Shane yawned but did not slow.

They shaved.

All of them.

Beards were removed carefully, not because they disliked them, but because their mother had said so.

Hair was trimmed clean. Shirts were freshly pressed. Work pants brushed and mended. Boots scrubbed until the leather shone, though they would be worn into dirt again before the day was done.

They looked like men ready to work.

They also looked like boys about to be hugged.

Breakfast was quick but warm—eggs, bread, coffee strong enough to steady nerves. Herbert Harvey stood at the head of the table, watching his sons with satisfaction.

"She has been gone six months," he said. "Do not forget yourselves."

"We won't," Sam replied.

"She will be tired," Herbert continued. "Do not overwhelm her."

"We won't," Seth echoed.

"And she will have luggage," Herbert said. "More than last time, I expect."

Scott nodded. "We've prepared wagons."

Three of them.

Herbert paused at that. "Three?"

"Yes, sir," Shane said. "She mentioned goods."

Herbert smiled faintly. "She always brings more than she needs."

"She always brings more than she left with," Scott said quietly.

That was true.

They loved their mother.

Deeply.

She had been the soft place where discipline rested. The one who laughed quietly when their father spoke firmly. The one who believed joy was not rebellion. The one who cooked with spice and story and music in her hands.

They missed her hugs.

They missed her voice calling them by name with warmth instead of instruction.

They missed the way she smelled like bread and citrus and something unexplainably alive.

Herbert cleared his throat. "We will go now."

They loaded the wagons—clean, sturdy, lined with blankets. They drove into town early, work waiting but postponed because obedience mattered more.

People noticed.

They always did when the Harvey men arrived together.

"Something special?" someone asked near the mercantile.

"Our mother is returning," Sam said simply.

That explained everything.

Back on the train, the conductor passed through.

"One hour, ladies."

Amy clasped her hands. "Lord."

Ana whispered, "We are ready."

Asha said softly, "Prepare the ground."

Hannah stood near the door now, heart steady, anticipation blooming. She had sent the telegram. She had made her requests. And for once in her life, she did not feel guilty for wanting a moment to be grand.

She thought of Herbert—upright, faithful, strict, loving in the ways he knew how. She thought of how he had asked her to give up dancing, believing it was obedience.

She smiled to herself.

She had not given it up.

She had simply waited.

The Stage Sisters gathered behind her, boots polished, dresses bright, hats feathered and unapologetic.

Abby leaned close. "Remember. You step off first."

Hannah nodded. "I know."

Amy whispered, "Thirty seconds."

Ana grinned. "Then we explode."

Hannah laughed softly. "You are outrageous."

"Yes," Abby said. "And intentional."

The train slowed.

The sound carried down the line into Stillwater Crossing, where wagons stood ready and six men waited with straight backs and nervous hands.

The whistle blew.

And nothing—absolutely nothing—would be the same again.

Chapter Six

Stillwater Crossing Receives the Unexpected

The train slowed with a long, deliberate sigh.

Metal against metal. Steam lifting. Wheels easing into place as if even the engine itself understood it was arriving somewhere that thought it knew what to expect.

The conductor's voice rang out, clear and official:

"Stillwater Crossing!"

On the platform, the **Harvey family** stood waiting.

Herbert Harvey was at the center—tall, broad, immaculately pressed, posture straight as a fence post. His hat sat low and proper. His hands were clasped behind his back, as if containing both anticipation and authority at once.

Beside and slightly behind him stood his six sons.

Six men, each over six feet tall. Broad-shouldered. Sun-browned. Muscled from honest labor. Their clean-shaven faces looked younger without the beards, almost startlingly so. Fresh haircuts sharpened their features. Crisp shirts. Clean work pants. Boots scrubbed within an inch of respectability.

They looked like a line of responsibility.

They also looked painfully shy.

Not toward their mother—never toward her—but toward the idea of women in general, which they tended to treat like sudden weather: unpredictable and best observed from a distance.

They expected solemnity.

They expected restraint.

They expected their mother to step down in a sensible dress, hair tied neatly back in a ribbon or bun, posture composed, expression calm and grateful.

They expected *homecoming*.

What they got was **Hannah**.

She stepped down from the train laughing.

Her long black hair flowed freely down her back, catching the light like something alive. Trinkets chimed softly at her ears and wrists. Bangles moved with her hands. Her dress brushed just above her ankles—intentionally—

and moved as she moved, not stiff, not cautious.

She looked ten years younger.

No—she *felt* ten years younger, and it showed.

Her face was radiant. Her eyes sparkled. Her whole body carried motion, as if she might twirl at any moment just because she could.

For one suspended second, no one breathed.

Herbert froze.

Not because she was beautiful—he knew that.

But because she was **outspoken**.

Visible.

Uncontained.

His ears warmed instantly. His chest tightened. A dozen thoughts collided: propriety, attention, witnesses, church members, townsfolk, sons—

Then instinct took over.

He stepped forward quickly and wrapped her into his arms, strong and encompassing, almost as if he were shielding her from the entire platform.

"Hannah," he said low, urgent, affectionate. "You're home."

He did not kiss her.

That, in his mind, was private.

Hannah smiled against his chest.

Then she did the unthinkable.

She leaned back, placed both hands on his shoulders, rose just enough on her toes—

—and kissed her husband **full on the mouth**.

Open. Certain. Unapologetic.

The platform collectively forgot how to exist.

Herbert stiffened in pure shock.

Then, to his own astonishment—

He kissed her back.

Fully.

Deeply.

Like a man who remembered something he had not allowed himself to remember in years.

A sharp chorus of throat-clearing erupted behind them.

Six sons.

All at once.

Loud.

Uncomfortable.

Horrified.

Sam stared at the sky.
Seth examined his boots.
Silas froze completely.
Saul swallowed hard.
Scott blinked rapidly.
Shane looked like he might pass out.

Herbert and Hannah slowly came apart, their foreheads resting together, eyes locked like the world had narrowed to just the two of them.

Herbert leaned in, voice barely audible.

"Hannah Harvey," he murmured in her ear, "I cannot wait to get you home."

She blushed—actually blushed—and laughed softly.

And then—

Color exploded.

From the train doors stepped a **procession of women** that looked like joy had decided to parade.

The **Stage Sisters** descended one by one.

Their boots were ankle-high and polished. Their dresses were vibrant—rich reds, deep blues, golds, greens. Some wore feathered hats. Others had flowers pinned just so. Stage makeup enhanced what was already striking—eyes bright, lips alive, smiles confident.

They didn't simply walk.

They **moved**.

Each step flowed into the next like choreography no one had rehearsed but everyone felt.

They came in different colors. Different shapes. Different presences.

They were not loud yet—but they were undeniable.

The men on the platform—every single one—stared.

Mouths parted.

Hats forgotten.

These were not call girls.

These were not saloon women.

These were something far more unsettling.

Sophisticated.

Alive.

Joyful without asking permission.

"HANNAH!" they called out together.

They rushed her in a wave of color and sound, arms wrapping around her, laughter spilling freely. They hugged her fiercely, kissed her cheeks, leaving playful red lipstick marks that Hannah didn't even try to wipe away.

She laughed—open, full-bodied, unashamed.

Then, right there on the platform, they began to dance.

Not wild.

Not indecent.

But **free**.

Hannah joined them.

Just a few steps.

A turn.

A laugh.

Her bangles chimed.

Some townspeople gasped.

Some clapped—tentative at first, then braver.

Others turned away sharply.

"Disgraceful," someone muttered.

"I never," said another, marching off.

The six Harvey sons stood frozen.

They had never seen women like this.

They had never seen their **mother** like this.

They were terrified.

Not of danger—but of proximity.

They could not even bring themselves to step forward.

Finally, the Stage Sisters eased away, breathless and smiling, and began managing luggage with practiced ease.

Trunks. Bags. Hat boxes. More than three wagons worth.

The Harvey sons still didn't move.

Hannah turned, hands on hips, radiant and commanding.

"Well?" she said. "Are you going to stand there all day?"

That broke the spell.

One by one, her sons came forward and hugged her—awkward, earnest, relieved. Each one held her a second longer than necessary, breathing her in like reassurance.

Then Hannah turned brisk.

"Put the luggage in the wagons," she ordered. "Take the women to the boardinghouse. See that they're comfortable."

The sons nodded immediately.

"Yes, ma'am."

"After that," she continued, "bring them home."

Their eyes widened.

Home?

"Yes," Hannah said firmly. "They are my guests."

She took the Stage Sisters' hands.

"Come with me," she said. "We'll check you in properly."

Before anyone could object, she added, "We will pray first."

They did.

Right there.

The men watched.

Silent. Awed. Unsure how to speak.

As the wagons began to load and movement resumed, Hannah caught the Stage Sisters' eyes.

She laughed.

And winked.

Stillwater Crossing had been waiting for a train.

It had just received a transformation.

Chapter Seven

Guests, Wagons, and the Trouble of Being Seen

The boardinghouse had never known a day like it.

Mrs. Wilkins, who had run the place for nearly twenty years with steady hands and cautious opinions, stood behind her front desk gripping a ledger she had suddenly forgotten how to use.

Hannah Harvey stood beside her, radiant and utterly unconcerned.

"These women are with me," Hannah said pleasantly. "They will need rooms. Good ones."

Mrs. Wilkins blinked. "All... all of them?"

"Yes," Hannah replied. "Together, if possible."

The Stage Sisters stood just behind her— relaxed, smiling, boots still dusty from the platform, hats tilted with confidence. They did not crowd. They did not rush. They simply existed, which somehow felt like the boldest thing of all.

"Well," Mrs. Wilkins said after a moment, clearing her throat, "we do have rooms. Upstairs. Three on each side."

"That will do nicely," Hannah said. "They prefer stairs."

Amy Stage leaned in cheerfully. "We like to earn our rest."

Mrs. Wilkins flushed, unsure whether that was encouragement or commentary.

The Harvey brothers stepped in without being asked.

"Where to?" Sam said.

"Rooms," Anne replied, handing over tags like a woman accustomed to being obeyed.

The men took luggage.

And immediately underestimated it.

"What *is* in here?" Saul muttered under his breath as he hoisted one trunk.

"Shoes," Abby answered sweetly.

"Just shoes?" Scott asked, straining.

"Mostly," Amy said. "With opinions."

Silas said nothing, simply adjusted his grip and carried on.

Up the stairs they went—boots thudding, trunks bumping, the sound echoing through the boardinghouse like a rumor traveling too fast to stop.

Downstairs, the women waited.

They sat together on the parlor settees, skirts arranged comfortably, laughter rising and falling naturally. Hannah stayed with them, pointing out windows, making small observations about town life, entirely unconcerned by the fact that more than one curtain across the street had begun to twitch.

Outside, the rumors had already grown legs.

By the time the Harvey men came back down the stairs, a small crowd had gathered near the front of the boardinghouse.

Men.

Some familiar. Some curious. Some openly annoyed.

"Those the women?" someone whispered loudly.

"They look like it," another replied.

A third scoffed. "And they're with the Harveys?"

Voices rose just enough to be sure they carried.

"Seems convenient."

"First choice, huh?"

"That's how it always goes."

Sam stopped at the door.

He turned slowly, posture straight, expression firm.

"We don't know the women," he said evenly. "They are guests of our mother."

A murmur rippled through the group.

"Your mother brought them?"

"Yes," Seth added. "On the train."

"Well," a man said, arms crossed, "that don't seem fair."

Anne Stage stepped forward then—not angry, not defensive—simply present.

"No one has been promised to anyone," she said calmly. "And no one has been taken."

Abby smiled beside her. "We just arrived."

The men didn't quite know how to respond to that.

Hannah appeared at the door, hands on hips, eyes bright.

"Is there a problem?" she asked pleasantly.

The crowd shifted.

"No, Mrs. Harvey," someone muttered.

"Good," Hannah said. "Because my guests are tired."

That ended it.

The wagons were brought around.

Two of them.

Clean, sturdy, lined with blankets.

The Stage Sisters stepped out into the sunlight like they had planned it.

They were even more flamboyant now—hats adjusted, skirts lifted just enough to step easily, boots polished, colors alive against the dust of Stillwater Crossing.

They smelled like soap and citrus and something warm and sweet—bread, spice, perfume made with intention.

Laughter followed them like a signature.

The Harvey brothers stood waiting, reins in hand, still not quite certain where to look.

Names were exchanged quickly.

"I'm Sam."

"Seth."

"Silas."

"Saul."

"Scott."

"Shane."

Each name offered plainly. Each received with a smile.

The women responded in turn, voices warm, eyes kind, entirely unafraid.

They climbed into the wagons, skirts arranged, laughter continuing.

As the wheels turned and the town fell behind them, the men rode in silence for a while.

They did not know how to speak.

Not because they lacked words—but because they had never practiced using them around women like this.

Finally, Scott cleared his throat.

"We raise cattle," he said.

Amy nodded enthusiastically. "Good protein."

Seth swallowed. "We grow wheat."

Ana smiled. "I see bread in your future."

Saul added stiffly, "We sell at market."

Anne inclined her head. "Wise."

Then silence again.

The Stage Sisters chatted softly among themselves, laughter like music. The men listened without meaning to.

The ranch came into view.

Hands stopped working.

Literally.

Ranch hands froze mid-step, mouths open, hats half-lifted, brooms forgotten.

Wagons full of women.

Bright women.

Laughing women.

The kind of women stories warned you about.

Hannah was having the time of her life.

She leaned across the wagon seat and kissed Herbert whenever she could reach him—on the cheek, the jaw, once dangerously close to his mouth again.

Herbert coughed.

"Not here," he murmured, flustered and smiling despite himself.

Hannah laughed. "You're home now."

The ranch, which had known only order and routine, held its breath.

And waited.

The Ranch and the Reckoning

The wagons rolled through the gates of the Harvey ranch just as the afternoon light softened the land, turning fields gold and fences kind. The place was quiet in the way of long-kept order—nothing out of place, nothing loud, nothing unexpected.

Until now.

The Stage Sisters stepped down first.

The Harvey men jumped down quickly, hands out, offering assistance before thinking too hard about it. Ankles touched dirt. Skirts brushed calloused fingers. Perfume drifted— warm, clean, alive.

Abby winked as Sam helped her down.

Amy looped her arm through Seth's without asking.
Ana laughed softly when Saul steadied her waist for half a second too long.
Asha thanked Silas with a nod that somehow made his ears burn.
Anne adjusted her skirt and met Scott's eyes calmly, which unsettled him more than flirtation ever could.
Shane nearly tripped helping Abby with a trunk and earned a grin that stayed with him longer than was reasonable.

They were escorted inside like men who had forgotten how doors worked.

The house was beautiful.

Not showy—solid.

Clean floors worn smooth by years of care. Wide halls. High ceilings. Light pouring in from generous windows. Fifteen bedrooms stretched through the house like quiet promise. Two kitchens—one for daily use, one for preserving and feeding many. Three tiled washrooms coiled neatly off the halls. Smokehouses stood outside, steady and fragrant with cured meat. Small houses dotted the edges of the land for ranch hands with families, and beyond them a large bunkhouse waited, currently very silent.

Everything spoke of provision.

And control.

The women took it in appreciatively.

"This house breathes," Amy said.

Ada nodded. "It has been respected."

Ana smiled. "And fed well."

They were deposited politely into the parlor—soft chairs, sturdy tables, Scripture framed neatly on the wall—then the brothers vanished.

Literally vanished.

One moment they were there, hats in hand, clearing throats.

The next, the house held only women and Hannah Harvey laughing like a woman newly unburdened.

"Oh, I adore this room," Abby said, spinning once before stopping herself. "I won't dance indoors. Yet."

Amy laughed. "Give it ten minutes."

Hannah waved a hand. "Sit. Rest. You've traveled."

They did.

And talked.

And laughed.

And rearranged themselves comfortably like they belonged.

Meanwhile, the six Harvey brothers were crammed into **Seth's bedroom**, standing, sitting, pacing, and breathing like men who had just survived a flood and were unsure the ground would hold.

"This is ungodly," Sam said finally.

Seth nodded sharply. "Absolutely."

"Rouge," Saul added, scandalized. "Lipstick."

"And ankles," Scott muttered. "Above them."

"Worse," Shane said faintly, "they dance."

Silas leaned against the wall, arms crossed. "They made Mother dance."

Silence fell.

"And," Seth added grimly, "she kissed Father. In public."

They all shuddered.

Sam ran a hand through his hair. "Men outside the boardinghouse were getting agitated."

"Yes," Saul said. "We nearly had words."

"And now," Scott said slowly, "Mother wants us to cook."

They stared at one another.

"Cook," Seth repeated.

110

"For them," Shane whispered.

"They are... extremely beautiful," Scott added helplessly.

"They smell," Shane said, searching for the right word, "like life."

Sam exhaled hard. "We need guidance."

Silas spoke at last. "We need Mother."

Right on cue, Hannah's voice rang down the hall.

"Boys!"

They flinched.

"Warm the food!" she called cheerfully. "Our guests are hungry."

A beat.

"And wash your hands!"

They looked at one another in horror.

"This is happening," Shane said weakly.

"Yes," Sam said, squaring his shoulders. "And we will behave like men."

They opened the door.

In the kitchen, the Stage Sisters had already begun to move—setting plates, opening lids, smiling knowingly.

Abby leaned against the counter. "There they are."

Amy grinned. "You disappeared."

Ana added warmly, "We thought we scared you."

Silas swallowed. "No, ma'am."

Asha smiled gently. "You don't need to be afraid."

That did not help.

Hannah stood at the stove, radiant, entirely at home.

"Come now," she said. "Serve."

The brothers moved like men walking into deep water.

Hands brushed.

Eyes met.

Laughter rang.

The Stage Sisters teased lightly—not cruelly, not aggressively—just enough to make them aware of themselves.

"Careful," Abby said to Sam as he handed her a plate. "You're blushing."

"I am not," Sam said stiffly.

Amy leaned close to Seth. "You cook well."

"Thank you," he said quickly, then froze. "I mean—you're welcome."

Hannah watched it all with delight.

Holy moly, indeed.

The ranch had never seen a day like this.

And the men of the house had absolutely no idea what they were going to do next.

Chapter Eight

Supper, Silence, and the Mercy of Sleep

By the time the pots were uncovered and the lids lifted, the Harvey kitchen no longer belonged to habit.

It belonged to motion.

The brothers moved in practiced order—one at the stove, one at the counter, one at the oven—warming dishes they had prepared earlier that morning with the same care they gave the land. Cast iron pans hissed softly. Steam rose fragrant and comforting. Bread was sliced thick. Butter melted without being asked.

The Stage Sisters did not hover.

They *helped*.

"Plates are here," Amy said cheerfully, opening a cupboard as if she had lived there all her life.

"Serving spoons?" Ana asked, already finding them.

"Napkins?" Abby called.

"Drawer beneath the bread box," Scott
answered automatically—then froze when he
realized he had spoken without thinking.

Abby smiled at him like a reward.

They brought the dishes out together, as if this
were the most natural thing in the world.

The table filled quickly.

Roast beef slow-cooked and tender. Potatoes
rich with butter and herbs. Corn simmered
sweet. Beans deep and savory. Pitchers of iced
tea sweating onto folded cloths. And at the
center—peach cobbler, golden and fragrant,
resting like a promise.

"This," Amy whispered reverently, "is holy
ground."

The brothers took their seats.

And somehow—without a word spoken about
it—the Stage Sisters each found their way to
the places they had already chosen.

Abby sat beside Sam.
Amy slid easily next to Seth.
Ana took Saul's side with a smile.
Asha sat near Silas, quiet and steady.
Anne chose Scott, eyes thoughtful.
Shane blinked twice when Abby passed him by
and then nearly forgot how chairs worked.

None of the men commented.

They were too busy attempting to breathe normally.

Upstairs, Hannah and Herbert remained in their room longer than expected.

They talked.

They laughed quietly.

They sat close, hands touching, rediscovering familiarity that had been buried under routine.

They were, for a little while, newlyweds again.

Downstairs, supper began.

Plates were passed. Heads bowed. Prayer spoken simply and sincerely by Sam, voice steady despite everything inside him racing.

"Amen," came softly from all sides.

Forks moved.

The food was magnificent.

The men knew it.

The women knew it.

No one said much.

116

The brothers ate with careful restraint, eyes mostly on their plates, words rationed like something precious. When spoken, they were brief.

"It's good," Seth said, clearing his throat.

"Thank you," Amy replied brightly. "We agree."

Silas nodded once when Asha complimented the seasoning. Saul nearly dropped his fork when Ana leaned close to ask for the butter. Scott forgot what he was saying mid-sentence when Anne asked him about the ranch books.

Shane stared at his plate as if it might betray him.

The women noticed.

They always did.

And they loved it.

Not cruelly.

Not to humiliate.

But because it was honest.

They teased lightly—just enough to invite reaction.

"Do you always eat so quietly?" Abby asked Sam sweetly.

"Yes, ma'am," he said immediately.

Amy tilted her head at Seth. "You look like you're trying not to smile."

"I am smiling," Seth said stiffly.

Ana laughed. "Your face disagrees."

The men endured it like men who had never been practiced at joy under observation.

Still, they did not retreat.

And that mattered.

By the time the last plates were cleared, relief settled in alongside satisfaction.

"Well," Abby said, stretching slightly, "that was delightful."

"And exhausting," Anne added.

"Yes," Asha said softly. "We have traveled far."

Hannah and Herbert joined them at last.

Hannah looked radiant. Herbert looked both proud and faintly overwhelmed.

They ate what remained, listened to fragments of conversation, and observed what was unfolding without comment.

After supper, everyone rose together.

Dishes were gathered.

Water heated.

And without discussion, the women and men worked side by side.

Plates washed. Cups dried. Counters wiped.

Hands brushed accidentally and were withdrawn immediately—then brushed again.

Hannah watched from her chair, smiling knowingly.

At last, she spoke.

"It is too late to travel back tonight."

The Stage Sisters nodded easily.

"We agree," Abby said. "We are grateful."

"You will stay," Hannah continued. "The spare rooms are ready."

No one argued.

She turned to her sons. "Bring extra pillows and blankets. Leave them outside the doors."

"Yes, Mother," came six voices at once.

"And do not enter the ladies' rooms," she added firmly.

The men nodded solemnly, grateful for clear instruction.

The pillows were delivered.

The blankets folded neatly.

Everything placed just so.

They gathered once more in the parlor.

Chairs drawn close.

Lamps dimmed.

Sam offered to pray again, but Hannah shook her head gently.

"I will," she said.

She prayed with warmth and authority, thanking God for safe travels, good food, unexpected fellowship, and rest. She asked for protection, peace, and wisdom for the days ahead.

"Amen," everyone murmured.

Hannah smiled. "Two of you boys will take the women back to the boardinghouse after breakfast."

"Yes, ma'am."

"Tomorrow will be full," she added. "Tonight, you sleep."

No one argued.

They were beyond words now.

The men were too tired to talk.

The women were too tired to tease.

Doors closed softly.

Lights dimmed.

The house settled.

And for the first time in a long while, the Harvey home slept under the weight of something new—quiet anticipation and the promise of tomorrow.

Dawn, Bread, and the First Blow

Dawn came quietly over the Harvey ranch, pale light easing through the windows as if careful not to disturb what had barely settled.

But the house was already awake.

Boots moved softly across floors. Aprons were tied. Sleeves rolled. Coffee was set to boil before anyone had to ask. Whatever shock and confusion had gripped the men the night before had not altered one truth: work was familiar, and morning was meant to be met upright.

The women were already in the kitchen when the men arrived.

Not hovering.

Working.

Amy was kneading dough with practiced confidence.
Ana had a skillet going, ham sizzling thick and fragrant.
Abby cracked eggs with one hand, laughing when a shell fought back.
Anne peeled potatoes efficiently, eyes sharp even at dawn.
Asha poured milk into pitchers and murmured a quiet prayer over the table.

Ada arranged plates neatly, movements precise and calming.

For a moment, the Harvey men simply stood there.

Then Sam cleared his throat. "What needs doing?"

Everything loosened after that.

Hands moved. Chairs scraped. Biscuits went into the oven. Coffee was poured—strong, dark, unapologetic. Butter softened. Milk chilled. Potatoes browned golden in rendered fat.

It was a **hearty breakfast**—the kind meant to steady men for long days and remind women they were welcome.

They sat together.

And this time, the silence felt different.

Less fear.

More gravity.

Biscuits split open and slathered with butter. Ham disappeared quickly. Eggs were devoured. Coffee cups were refilled without asking.

Abby smiled at Sam. "You cook like someone raised right."

Sam flushed. "Thank you, ma'am."

Amy leaned toward Seth. "If you ever stop looking like you're being tested, this will be enjoyable."

Seth swallowed. "I am... enjoying myself."

Ana laughed softly. "We can tell."

Afterward, cleanup happened fast and natural—no awkwardness now, just tired cooperation. Plates washed. Counters wiped. Floors swept.

Hannah entered last, glowing, hair pinned loosely, eyes bright with private laughter.

"Well," she said, surveying the room, "that was successful."

Herbert kissed her cheek without thinking.

Everyone noticed.

Everyone pretended not to.

Hannah clapped once. "Now. Two of you boys—wagons."

Sam and Scott stepped forward immediately.

"Yes, Mother."

She turned to the women, taking their hands one by one. "I will visit soon. But for now, I need time with my husband."

Amy grinned. "We understand."

Abby winked. "Completely."

Hannah laughed, hugged them tightly, and prayed with them again—firm, warm, protective.

"God goes with you," she said. "And He is not surprised by what He brings."

The wagons rolled out shortly after.

Sam and Scott drove.

The ride back toward town was almost silent.

Not awkward.

Heavy.

The Stage Sisters spoke quietly among themselves.

"An acre each," Anne murmured. "That's manageable."

"And an abandoned building," Ana said. "Something with bones."

"A bakery," Amy added. "First thing."

"And the studio," Abby said softly. "It has to exist."

Asha nodded. "Yes."

The men listened without comment, eyes forward.

The boardinghouse came into view.

Something felt wrong immediately.

Too quiet.

Too many eyes.

As they pulled up, **Mrs. Wilkins** stood rigid at the door, hands folded tightly in front of her. Her face was pale. Behind her, the parlor was visible—

And every single trunk, bag, hat box, and case the women owned was piled there.

Carelessly.

Like something removed in haste.

Amy's breath caught. "Why is our luggage... there?"

Mrs. Wilkins cleared her throat. "Ladies."

Abby stepped down. "What happened?"

Mrs. Wilkins looked at the ground. "Some of the men... stayed up last night."

Anne stiffened. "Watching what?"

"The house," Mrs. Wilkins said quietly. "They noticed you did not return."

Sam frowned. "That is none of their concern."

"Well," she continued, voice tight, "they decided it was."

Ana's voice trembled. "What did they say?"

Mrs. Wilkins swallowed. "That ungodly things must have occurred."

The words landed like stones.

"They said," Mrs. Wilkins went on, "that respectable women do not spend the night away without... consequence."

Amy's eyes filled instantly. "We were guests."

"Yes," Mrs. Wilkins said. "I told them that."

Abby's jaw set. "And?"

"And they went to the church," she said softly. "Early. Before sunrise."

Anne felt her stomach drop. "Who?"

"The religious women," Mrs. Wilkins said. "They complained to the Reverend."

Sam's fists clenched. "About what?"

"That the Harvey brothers," she said carefully, "should not attend service until they make right by you."

Scott's face drained of color. "Make right?"

"By marrying you," Mrs. Wilkins finished.

Silence.

Thick.

Horrified.

Amy whispered, "We didn't do anything."

Asha's hands shook. "We prayed."

Abby's voice broke. "This is wicked."

Mrs. Wilkins nodded. "It gets worse."

The men leaned in.

"The local men," she said, "think this improves their chances with the bridal train women if the Harvey boys are... removed."

Anne went cold. "They want them shamed out."

"Yes."

Sam closed his eyes briefly. "This is because of us."

Abby turned sharply. "No."

Ana's tears spilled. "We didn't mean—"

Scott interrupted, voice firm. "This is not your fault."

But the damage had already begun.

The Stage Sisters stood in the parlor, staring at their lives stacked like baggage someone else had judged.

Amy sank onto a chair and sobbed openly.
Ana covered her mouth.
Asha closed her eyes, praying through tears.
Abby stared at the wall, furious and helpless.
Anne's hands trembled as she counted possibilities that no longer existed.
Ada stood still—perfectly still—absorbing the blow with quiet dignity.

"We have nowhere," Amy whispered.

Abby swallowed hard. "We won't cause trouble."

Anne nodded. "We'll wait."

"For the next train," Ana said brokenly.

Asha whispered, "The bridal train.in a few days"

Silence again.

Sam moved first.

"Load them," he said to Scott, voice tight. "Carefully."

Scott nodded. "We'll take what we can now."

They worked fast.

Too fast.

Trunks lifted. Bags secured. Women helped with shaking hands.

Tears fell into wagon boards.

As they settled in, Abby finally broke.

"This isn't fair," she cried. "We didn't do anything wrong."

Sam couldn't look at her. "I know."

Amy clutched Ana's hand. "We don't want to hurt your family."

Scott's voice cracked. "You already haven't."

The wagons rolled away again—slow, heavy, hearts breaking under the weight of judgment.

Behind them, Stillwater Crossing stood quietly righteous.

Ahead of them, uncertainty waited.

And somewhere on the rails, a bridal train was coming.

Dust, Tears, and Hannah Harvey's Private Satisfaction

The wagon wheels creaked softly as they rolled back toward the ranch, but the sound was nearly swallowed by sobbing.

Not delicate tears.

The kind that came from shock, humiliation, and the sudden understanding that goodness did not always protect you from being misjudged.

Abby sat rigid, staring straight ahead, jaw tight as stone.
Amy cried openly, shoulders shaking.
Ana pressed a hand to her chest, whispering prayers through tears.
Asha rocked gently, eyes closed, lips moving constantly.
Anne wiped her face angrily, furious at herself for not anticipating this.
Ada sat upright, dignified even in grief, eyes shining but unbroken.

"We were judged," Amy sobbed. "Unfairly."

"And quickly," Anne added. "No trial. No listening."

Ana shook her head. "We brought trouble to good people."

Abby's voice broke. "That is what hurts the most."

Sam and Scott said nothing. Their hands were tight on the reins. Their shoulders were rigid with a shame they had not earned but felt deeply.

"We didn't come to marry," Amy said through tears. "We came to *build*."

"Yes," Anne said. "Land. Work. Community."

"Bread," Ana whispered.

"And dance," Abby said softly. "Healing."

Asha's voice was steady even as tears slipped down her face. "They quoted Scripture."

Sam flinched. "Which ones?"

Asha swallowed. "They said '*shun the appearance of evil.*'"

Scott muttered, "They always use that one."

"And '*it is better to marry than to burn,*'" Asha continued. "As if marriage is a punishment for proximity."

Ana let out a bitter laugh. "They said it was to protect the children."

Amy sniffed. "From ankles?"

Abby wiped her face. "From joy."

Anne's voice hardened. "From women who don't shrink."

They all fell silent then, grief settling deeper.

"We should leave," Abby said at last. "As soon as possible."

"Yes," Amy nodded. "We'll wait for the next train."

Ana whispered, "We'll dust the dust off our feet."

Asha quoted softly, "*If they do not receive you... shake the dust from your feet.*"

Ada nodded once. "We will not fight them."

Sam finally spoke, voice strained. "You are not the ones who should leave."

Abby turned sharply. "But we are the ones causing harm."

Scott swallowed hard. "You didn't cause this."

"But we *triggered* it," Anne said. "And now your family is being punished."

The wagon stopped.

They had reached the ranch.

The wide, familiar land stretched out before them—peaceful, steady, innocent of what had just unfolded.

The women did not move.

"I can't go in," Amy whispered. "I'm too embarrassed."

Abby nodded. "We'll stay here."

Ana clasped her hands. "We don't want to disturb Hannah."

"And her husband," Asha added gently.

Scott hesitated. "She'll notice."

Abby shook her head. "Please. Give us a moment."

The brothers exchanged a look.

Then Sam nodded. "We'll tell her."

They stepped down and walked toward the house.

The women remained in the wagons.

They prayed.

135

Out loud.

Through tears.

"Lord," Ana cried, "we didn't mean to cause division."

Amy sobbed, "We only wanted to work and live."

Asha whispered, "Cover this family. Do not let them be harmed because of us."

Abby pressed her fists to her eyes. "We don't even want marriage right now. We just want purpose."

Anne said bitterly, "They didn't ask us what we wanted."

Ada spoke quietly, firmly. "We know who we are."

Inside the house, Sam and Scott stood stiffly before their parents.

Hannah took one look at their faces and knew.

"Oh," she said softly. "So it's begun."

Herbert frowned. "What's wrong?"

"The town," Scott said. "The church."

Sam added, "They've judged the women. And us."

Hannah's lips twitched.

"Go on," she said calmly.

They explained everything—boardinghouse gossip, religious women, Scripture wielded like a club, the threat of church discipline, the bridal train strategy.

Herbert's jaw tightened. "This is improper."

"Yes," Hannah agreed. "Improperly handled."

She rose immediately.

"Where are they?"

"In the wagons," Sam said. "Crying."

Hannah did not rush.

She smoothed her dress.

Adjusted her scarf.

And smiled to herself.

This, she thought, is better than I imagined.

She stepped outside.

The sight stopped the women's sobbing instantly.

Hannah stood there, hands on hips, eyes bright—not angry. Not distressed.

Amused.

"Alright," she said. "That is enough."

Abby gasped. "Hannah—"

"Inside," Hannah ordered gently. "All of you."

"We don't want—" Amy began.

"I said inside," Hannah repeated, voice warm but immovable.

They obeyed.

As they climbed down, Hannah walked behind them, her smile deepening with every step.

Six women.
Six sons.
Six misunderstandings.

And six solutions.

She glanced toward the fields where the other sons worked, blissfully unaware.

"Oh," Hannah murmured to herself, "this is going to be magnificent."

Inside the house, she gathered them close.

"You have been humiliated," she said plainly. "Unjustly."

They nodded, ashamed.

"You have been accused," she continued. "Wrongly."

They wept again.

"And you are worried about my family," she finished.

"Yes," Abby whispered.

Hannah clasped her hands and looked heavenward briefly.

Then she smiled—bright, confident, utterly unrepentant.

"Well," she said, "the Reverend may think he has an opinion."

The women looked up.

"And the religious ladies may think they have authority."

Hannah leaned in conspiratorially.

"I will agree with them."

Gasps.

"But," Hannah continued sweetly, "I will do it *my way.*"

She straightened.

"In my mind," she thought happily, **I will attend six weddings very shortly.**

Six dancing daughters-in-law.

Six bold women who would turn Stillwater Crossing upside down.

And six shy sons who would learn—very quickly—that God was far more creative than their doctrine allowed.

Hannah clasped her hands.

"Now," she said brightly, "dry your faces. We have planning to do."

Chapter Nine

Work, Whispers, and a Dangerous Thought

The sun climbed higher over the fields, but the air did not lighten.

Out among the cattle and rows of feed, the Harvey brothers worked side by side as they always had—movements practiced, quiet, efficient. Boots pressed earth. Hands lifted tools. Muscles remembered purpose even when minds were elsewhere.

Sam and Scott approached from the lane.

They did not call out.

They didn't need to.

Something in their posture told the others this was not a casual interruption.

Seth straightened first. "What happened?"

Silas leaned on his shovel. Saul wiped his hands on his trousers. Shane paused mid-step, already sensing the weight of it.

Scott spoke. "The town."

That single word carried enough meaning to still the field.

Sam continued, voice low but steady. "Men were watching the boardinghouse last night."

Seth's jaw tightened. "Watching what?"

"Nothing," Sam said. "Which didn't stop them."

"They went to the church," Scott added. "Early. With stories."

Silas frowned. "Stories?"

Saul's eyes narrowed. "About us?"

"Yes," Sam said. "About the women. About Mother."

Shane swallowed. "What kind of stories?"

Scott answered bluntly. "That we behaved ungodly. That we shouldn't attend church until we 'make it right.'"

A sharp stillness fell.

"Make it right how?" Seth asked, though he already knew.

"Marriage," Sam said. "They're saying we should marry the women."

Shane let out a short, incredulous breath. "What?"

"And," Scott added, "that keeping us out of church improves other men's chances with the bridal train women."

The shovel slipped from Silas's hands and hit the dirt.

"They're trying to ruin our names," Saul said quietly.

"And not because we did anything," Seth added.

Sam nodded. "Exactly."

They stood there, the field suddenly too open, too exposed.

Scott spoke again. "The women are distraught. They think they've harmed our family."

Shane's voice cracked. "They haven't."

Silas spoke slowly. "Religion can do harm when it forgets mercy."

Seth nodded. "We know that."

Saul exhaled. "We're innocent."

"Yes," Sam said. "But innocence doesn't always protect you."

They fell silent, each man wrestling with the same truth.

Finally, Seth scoffed. "I don't want those bridal train women anyway."

Shane blinked. "You don't?"

"No," Seth said firmly. "They sound like a committee."

Saul snorted. "Supervised meetings?"

Scott shook his head. "We're not shopping for wives."

Sam said quietly, "We're keeping the ranch alive."

Silas added, "And we wouldn't miss church lightly."

Shane kicked at the dirt. "But we might."

All eyes turned to him.

"If we go," he continued, "they'll stare. Judge. Whisper."

"And if we don't," Saul said, "they'll say that proves something."

Seth ran a hand over his face. "This is how harm spreads."

Sam nodded. "Misguided righteousness."

They worked in silence for a few minutes after that, hands busy, thoughts racing.

Finally, Sam said, "We'll work until sundown. Then we'll pray. Then we'll speak to Mother and Father."

"Yes," Seth agreed. "After prayer."

They bowed their heads right there in the field.

No show.

No loud words.

Just steady faith.

"Lord," Sam prayed, "we ask You to cover the Stage Sisters."

"To guard their hearts," Seth added.

"And ours," Silas said.

"Do not let lies take root," Saul whispered.

"Give us wisdom," Scott said.

"And courage," Shane added softly.

They lifted their heads.

The field was quiet again.

Then Shane spoke.

"What if," he said slowly, "we took a chance?"

The others turned toward him.

"What if," Shane continued, heart pounding but voice steady, "we married them?"

Silence hit like thunder.

Seth stared. "You can't be serious."

Shane swallowed. "Mom already likes them."

"That's not—" Saul began.

"Dad has already met them," Shane pressed on. "Really met them."

Scott frowned. "We barely know them."

"And yet," Shane said, "we can't stop thinking about them."

Silas looked away. "They are... remarkable."

"They're bold," Shane continued. "Determined. They look like women who don't need men to survive."

Sam exhaled slowly. "That's what scares you? "Shane nodded. "Yes."

Seth scoffed weakly. "Can we get any prettier women?"

No one laughed.

"Someone else will marry them," Shane said quietly. "Look at the crowd outside the boardinghouse. We almost had a fight."

Saul rubbed his jaw. "He's not wrong."

Scott looked thoughtful. "They'll be snapped up."

"And then," Shane said, "we'll have caused harm *and* lost something we didn't know we wanted."

The men stood there, stunned—not by fear, but by possibility.

Sam spoke last. "This would take courage."

"Yes," Shane said. "God's courage."

They returned to their work, but the rhythm was altered now.

A thought had been planted.

And it refused to stay buried.

Chapter Nine

Ovens Warm, Intentions Warmer

Back at the house, the women did what women often do when hearts are bruised and words feel dangerous.

They worked.

The kitchen came alive early—fire lit, sleeves rolled, hair pinned back with purpose. Flour dusted the counters like quiet snowfall. Bowls clinked. Spoons scraped. The smell of yeast, sugar, butter, and spice filled the house until even the walls seemed to lean in closer.

"At least," Abby said, setting a pan into the oven with more force than necessary, "we can feed them well."

Amy nodded, eyes red but determined. "If we've brought harm, we'll bring supper too."

Ana wiped her face with her apron and smiled bravely. "Bread heals a lot of misunderstandings."

Asha murmured, "And prayer covers what bread can't."

They prayed as they worked—softly, steadily—asking for mercy, wisdom, and protection over a family they had come to care for far too quickly.

Hannah moved among them, calm and purposeful, offering guidance without interruption.

"Sugar's in the left jar," she said gently.
"Pies need time," she reminded.
"Don't rush the cake," she added with a knowing smile.

Inside, she was laughing to herself.

Six weddings soon.
Grandchildren tumbling through fields.
Dance halls breathing again.
Bakeries, sewing shops, and laughter on Main Street.

Oh, this was unfolding beautifully.

Her shy sons—oh yes—were already undone.

Outwardly, Hannah was all composure and agreement.

"You know," she said thoughtfully as the women worked, "the Reverend may be right about one thing."

Six heads turned.

"We should avoid the appearance of evil," Hannah continued soberly. "I should have thought of that last night."

Abby's shoulders sagged. "We didn't mean—"

"I know," Hannah said quickly, patting her arm. "Intentions matter. But appearances... they carry weight here."

Amy swallowed. "We never thought—"

Hannah nodded sympathetically. "And now my sons not being received at church will distress them deeply."

The women's faces fell.

Ana whispered, "We never wanted that."

"I know," Hannah said gently. "It brings a seeming disgrace to our family."

She let the words hang just long enough to sting—then softened.

"But we will weather this."

Herbert appeared at the doorway then, sleeves rolled, face thoughtful.

"We've weathered worse," he said calmly.

Hannah smiled at him, just slightly.

He knew.

They had talked.

He knew exactly what she was doing—and he was letting her.

The Stage Sisters absorbed the words like a sentence, not a strategy.

"We should make it right," Anne said firmly, already calculating dishes. "A proper meal."

"Yes," Abby agreed. "Something generous."

"Something beautiful," Amy added.

They went to work with renewed focus.

Hams glazed. Vegetables roasted. Bread baked fresh. A cake rose golden in the oven, and pies—apple and berry—cooled on racks, shining and fragrant.

"We'll show gratitude," Ana said. "Respect."

"And humility," Asha added softly.

Hannah watched them with affection.

If only you knew, she thought.

The house filled with warmth and anticipation—food as offering, labor as apology.

Outside, the sun dipped lower.

In the fields, six men worked toward evening with thoughts heavy and courage growing.

And in the kitchen, between prayer and pie crust, a mother quietly prepared to turn Stillwater Crossing upside down—one marriage, one dance step, one loaf of bread at a time.

Chapter Ten

Bread, Prayer, and the Decision No One Planned

The Harvey brothers came in just before dusk.

They had washed in the outdoor wash area, sleeves rolled, faces scrubbed until their cheeks were red and clean. Their hair was still damp, combed back with water and effort. They wore fresh shirts—simple, well kept— and work pants brushed free of field dust. Boots were left neatly by the door.

They stepped inside as one.

And stopped.

The house smelled like heaven had decided to settle down for supper.

Ham glazed and caramelized. Bread still warm. Butter melting. Spices blooming in the air. Fruit and sugar and cinnamon braided together into something that made the stomach ache with anticipation.

Scott inhaled slowly.
Shane whispered, "Mercy."
Seth closed his eyes for half a second.

No one spoke.

They were ready for anything.

But not for this.

The table was set long and generous. Platters gleamed. Pitchers of iced tea sweated onto cloth. Plates waited patiently, as if confident they would not be empty long.

Hannah stood at the head of the room, radiant and composed. Herbert sat nearby, calm, watchful.

The Stage Sisters stood together—not timid, not bold—simply present.

Hannah spoke first.

"We will eat," she said. "Then we will talk."

No one argued.

Grace was prayed—slow, sincere, steady.

And then forks moved.

Conversation was minimal. Not strained— reverent. As if everyone understood that this meal mattered.

The men ate like men who had worked all day and deserved rest. The women ate like women who had poured heart into labor and were finally sitting down.

Plates were refilled.

Seconds were taken.

The cake was admired.

The pies were cut carefully.

By the time dishes were cleared and water warmed for washing, something heavy had settled into peace.

They cleaned together again—quietly, efficiently—until counters shone and hands were dry.

Then they gathered.

Chairs pulled into a circle.

No table between them now.

Hannah folded her hands.

Herbert nodded once.

"Let us pray," Hannah said.

They bowed their heads.

Sam prayed this time. His voice was steady but earnest.

"Lord, You see our hearts. You know we did not intend harm. Give us wisdom now, and courage to do what is right. Not what is easy. Amen."

"Amen," came softly from every mouth.

Silence followed.

It was broken by the youngest.

Shane cleared his throat.

Everyone turned to him.

"I... I have something to say," he began, voice tight but determined. "I don't know what else to do."

Hannah kept her face neutral.

Herbert's brows lifted slightly.

Shane continued. "The town won't listen. The church has already decided. They won't receive us freely again unless this is... resolved."

Abby inhaled sharply.

Shane swallowed. "We discussed it in the field."

All eyes moved to the other brothers.

They did not deny it.

"If," Shane said, heart pounding now, "if the women would consider marrying us... then we could return to church freely."

A hush fell.

"We don't know another way," Shane added quickly. "And we don't want to shame our family."

Sam spoke next. "We talked. All of us."

Seth nodded. "We would take tomorrow off."

Saul added, "Go into town."

Scott said quietly, "Be married."

Silas finished, voice calm. "If they are willing."

Shane looked at the women then, earnest and unguarded.

"Where else would we find women this beautiful?" he said simply.

Hannah had to press her lips together.

Inside, she was laughing so hard she nearly burst.

This was better than anything she could have planned.

Quicker.

Cleaner.

God was efficient.

She also saw the logic unfolding clearly.

The women could still build. But now they would have land, labor, and standing.

Her sons would not be isolated. They would be stretched.

No one would starve.

No one would be silenced.

And Stillwater Crossing would never recover.

Herbert cleared his throat.

"Well," he said solemnly, "this is... serious."

Hannah nodded gravely, though her eyes danced.

"Yes," she said. "Marriage is not a solution to gossip."

The brothers nodded obediently.

"But," Hannah added gently, "it *can* be a covenant when entered wisely."

The Stage Sisters had gone very still.

Abby spoke first. "May we... have a moment?"

"Yes," Hannah said at once. "Take whatever time you need."

The women rose together and stepped outside.

The door closed softly behind them.

The evening air was cool. The fields stretched wide and forgiving. Crickets had begun their steady chorus.

They gathered in a loose circle.

Silence held for a breath.

Then Amy laughed—soft and incredulous.

"We did not come here to get married."

"No," Anne agreed. "We came to build."

Abby exhaled. "But we did bring trouble."

Ana nodded, eyes shining. "Not intentionally."

Asha spoke gently. "But impact matters."

They bowed their heads.

"We placed injustice upon this family," Amy whispered.

"And they're paying for it," Abby said.

Anne crossed her arms thoughtfully. "What would we actually lose?"

Ana smiled faintly. "The men are kind."

"And handsome," Amy added.

Abby laughed. "Very shy."

"Which can be taught," Anne said dryly.

Asha smiled. "They listen."

"They need work," Abby said, grinning. "In speech. Conversation. Dancing."

They all laughed quietly.

"And can we do better," Ana added softly, "than Hannah and Herbert as in-laws?"

Silence settled again.

This time, peaceful.

They prayed again—this time not out of distress, but clarity.

When they lifted their heads, Abby spoke.

"We can marry them."

Amy nodded. "Yes."

Anne added, "On our terms."

Ana smiled. "And then we build."

Asha said simply, "And we do good."

Abby's eyes sparkled. "We'll turn this town upside down with kindness."

They laughed together—bold, united, resolved.

They returned inside.

Hannah looked up.

And knew.

Her smile was radiant.

"Well?" she asked.

Abby stepped forward.

"We will marry them," she said.

"But," Anne added calmly, "we will also build."

Hannah clasped her hands.

"Oh," she said softly, "this is going to be wonderful."

Morning, Vows, and Six Very Determined Brides

Morning did not wait for anyone's nerves.

It arrived early, pale and confident, slipping through the Harvey house as if it had an appointment it intended to keep. Before the rooster could finish announcing himself, the kitchen was already alive.

The Stage Six rose together.

No discussion.
No debate.
Just purpose.

Aprons were tied. Sleeves rolled. Hair pinned back temporarily—*temporarily*, being the important word.

Abby set the griddle heating.
Amy mixed batter like it owed her money.
Ana warmed syrup and preserves, humming a tune that sounded suspiciously like joy.
Asha cracked eggs with calm precision.
Anne laid out plates and counted portions.
Ada moved between them all, adjusting, refining, making sure everything was beautiful and efficient.

Griddle cakes puffed golden, stacked high.
Syrup glistened. Preserves—peach, berry, and apple—were opened generously. Eggs

scrambled soft. Ham sliced thick and browned just enough to make a man reconsider every life decision that had led him to restraint.

Coffee was brewed strong enough to raise the dead—or at least wake the terrified.

By the time the Harvey brothers entered the kitchen, freshly washed and already nervous, the table looked like a feast prepared for conquest.

"Sit," Abby said cheerfully.

They did.

They ate.

And ate.

And ate.

Seth leaned back at one point, hand on his stomach. "I may not survive."

Amy smiled sweetly. "That's love."

Sam swallowed another bite. "How is it possible for food to do this?"

Ana laughed. "Intention."

Scott muttered, "I feel... undone."

Shane whispered, "I think I love breakfast."

The women exchanged glances, satisfied.

If marriage required courage, nourishment was clearly step one.

Afterward, dishes were washed and dried in brisk silence. No teasing now. No lingering looks. Everyone knew the next step required composure.

"Dress," Hannah said simply.

The house scattered.

The men emerged first.

Sunday clothing. Pressed shirts. Clean trousers. Boots polished to near-reflection. Hair neatly combed. Faces freshly shaved. They looked like men stepping into a photograph they hadn't practiced for.

The women came next.

And the air changed.

Stage finery. Rich colors. Dresses that moved when they moved. Makeup applied with intention—accentuating eyes, warming cheeks, lips bold and unapologetic. Hair styled to be seen.

The men stopped breathing.

Literally.

Sam froze.
Seth forgot where his hands went.
Silas swallowed hard.
Saul stared at the floor, then the ceiling, then anywhere but directly at Anne.
Scott looked like he might pass out.
Shane whispered, "Lord, help me."

Hannah and Herbert stepped in together then—hands linked, smiles soft, dressed like a couple rediscovering delight. They looked, unmistakably, like newlyweds who had remembered themselves.

Hannah surveyed the room.

Perfect.

The wagons were brought around.

Women seated carefully. Men mounted stiffly. The short ride to the parsonage passed in a blur of dust, pounding hearts, and prayers whispered under breath.

The Harvey ranch hand had already delivered the message.

Six marriages.
Paperwork prepared.
Immediately.

The Reverend had laughed quietly when he heard.

"Finally," he had murmured to himself. "The Lord is faithful."

He had prayed with Hannah for years—quiet prayers, hopeful prayers, specific prayers for wives who would strengthen, not diminish, her sons.

"Trust in the Lord with all your heart," he whispered, recalling Proverbs.
"He makes all things beautiful in His time."

When the wagons arrived, the Reverend stepped outside.

And stopped.

The women were... astonishing.

Not improper.
Not careless.
Alive.

He adjusted his glasses and smiled slowly.

"Well," he said under his breath, "Stillwater will not recover."

Inside, the paperwork waited neatly stacked.

The family filed in.

The Reverend greeted them warmly. Then, finally, his eyes met the brides.

He blinked once.

Twice.

"My," he said kindly, "you are... radiant."

Abby smiled. "Thank you, Reverend."

He cleared his throat. "I understand you are dancers."

"Yes," Amy said. "Among other things."

He nodded. "God is creative."

"Who can fathom the works of the Lord?" he quoted softly from Psalms.

The men stood beside their chosen wives, stiff as fence posts but determined.

Names were called.

One by one.

Each answered clearly.

"Do you accept one another?" the Reverend asked.

"Yes," came six voices.

Strong. Certain.

The Reverend lifted his hands. "By the authority vested in me, I pronounce you husband and wife."

Relief washed through the room.

Then he smiled.

"You may kiss the bride."

The men leaned in—hesitant, careful—aiming for cheeks.

The Stage Six had anticipated this.

Each woman turned at the exact right moment.

Six kisses landed squarely on lips.

Not scandalous.

Decisive.

Joyful.

The room gasped.

The men froze.

Then—slowly—kissed back.

Hannah laughed softly.

Oh yes.

Stillwater Crossing had no idea what it had just married into existence.

Hannah knew it the moment the words were spoken.

Not when the Reverend lifted his hands.
Not when the signatures were set in ink.
Not even when six kisses landed squarely where no one in Stillwater expected them to.

She knew it **right after**.

Right after the couples said *I do*.

Something shifted.

Not dramatic. Not loud.

But real.

Her sons—her reserved, disciplined, orderly sons—**transpired**.

They exhaled.

They stepped closer.

They started talking.

Actual talking.

Sam leaned toward Ada, voice low, surprised at himself.
"So... you really weren't afraid."

Ada smiled, steady and warm.
"I learned a long time ago that fear wastes time."

Sam nodded slowly. "I like that."

Seth laughed—a real laugh—as Ana adjusted his collar without asking.
"You smell like cinnamon," he said.

Ana grinned.
"I cook with joy. It lingers."

"Well," Seth said, clearing his throat, "I'd like it to linger... often."

Silas spoke quietly to Asha as they stood slightly apart from the others.
"I don't say much."

Asha smiled softly.
"I hear deeply."

Silas swallowed. "That feels... safe."

Saul was already blushing as Anne leaned close to him, voice calm and amused. "You're very serious."

Saul nodded.
"Yes, ma'am."

Anne tilted her head.
"You can stop calling me that."

He tried. Failed. Tried again.
"Anne."

Her smile rewarded the effort.

Scott looked dazed as Amy looped her arm through his.
"You okay?"

He shook his head slowly.
"No. But I think this is the best kind of not okay."

Shane—youngest, boldest—was already undone as Abby leaned in and whispered, "Well, husband... looks like we surprised the town."

He swallowed hard.
"I think we surprised ourselves."

Hannah pressed a hand to her mouth.

Lord, she thought, *they're alive.*

Someone had told the town.

Of course they had.

By the time the couples stepped outside the church, paperwork completed and a generous offering pressed warmly into the Reverend's hands, the crowd had grown.

Men stood shoulder to shoulder.
Women whispered behind gloved hands.
Children craned their necks.

Then clapping broke out.

First hesitant.

Then louder.

Especially from the men.

"Well I'll be," one said.
"Didn't expect that," said another.
"Good for them," someone muttered begrudgingly.

The newly married couples stepped into the light.

Six men.
Six women.
Different colors.
Different rhythms.
Now bound.

Hannah lifted her chin and spoke clearly.

"There will be a **celebration** on Saturday," she announced.
"A proper one."

Murmurs spread.

"We will celebrate my children," she continued, smiling broadly, "and I want to thank this town for helping make these weddings a reality."

She laughed suddenly, delighted.
"I might just kiss you all."

The crowd chuckled—nervous, uncertain, but disarmed.

Behind her, Herbert watched quietly.

He saw what Hannah saw.

His sons—arms now resting at waists instead of stiffly at sides. Heads leaned close. Voices lowered. Blushes blooming.

Sam breathed in Ada's perfume, startled by how grounding it felt.
Seth whispered something to Ana that made her laugh and nudge him.
Silas listened as Asha spoke, really listened.
Saul found himself smiling without guarding it.

Scott forgot to be restless.
Shane forgot to be afraid.

Hannah felt her eyes sting.

Oh, what a day.

Oh, what a night it will be.

They walked together into town, stopping first
at the **mercantile** to gather supplies for the
wedding dinner. Flour. Sugar. Meat. Produce.
Candles. Fabric.

The shopkeeper blinked repeatedly.

"Busy day," Hannah said cheerfully.

"Yes, ma'am," he replied weakly.

By the time wagons were loaded again,
Hannah was already giving instructions.

She had ranch hands preparing the **empty
cottages**—small homes scattered across the
land, once meant for extended family or
seasonal workers.

"They'll need space," she said.
"And privacy."

Beds were aired. Floors swept. Fires laid.
Curtains shaken out and food rations for three
days.

Each couple would have their own place—for now and not be to work or three full days.

"If they want to live in the big house later," Hannah said thoughtfully, "we'll see."

But for now, this was right.

The couples barely noticed.

They were too busy discovering one another affectionately, very affectionately without shame.

Hands held openly. Kissed often.
Words spoken easily.
Laughter unguarded.

Lunch was forgotten in the main house was forgotten.

Dinner loomed like a promise, but in small cottages

Hannah watched it all unfold with a joy so deep it bordered on awe.

Children would come soon, she thought.

Different colors.
Different gifts.
Different steps.

And her sons—oh, her sons—were already learning.

Whatever they lacked in ease or expression, she suspected these women were more than capable of teaching them.

She laughed aloud then, unable to contain it.

Just yesterday, they were strangers on a train.

And now—

"Hallelujah," Hannah whispered.

Stillwater Crossing had no idea what had just begun.

Chapter Eleven: Three Days Missing

No one at the Harvey Ranch saw the newly married couples for three full days.

Not the ranch hands.
Not the neighbors.
Not even the brothers' own kin.

Six cottages sat quiet at the edge of the land, smoke curling lazily from chimneys, doors firmly shut, curtains drawn—not in secrecy, but in **sanctuary**. Provisions had been stocked ahead of time: baskets of bread, jars of preserves, smoked meat, coffee strong enough to wake the dead, and enough blankets to last through winter if necessary.

Inside those cottages, marriages were being properly introduced to themselves spiritually and very much physically as husband and wives.

Cottage One

"You mean to tell me," one wife said slowly, sitting cross-legged on the bed, "that you have owned this ranch for ten years and never once sat still long enough to eat soup before it went cold?"

Her husband looked genuinely offended. "I eat efficiently."

She stared at him. "You stood up while chewing."

"Because the soup was hot."

She laughed, full-bodied and unashamed. "Lord help me. I married a man who doesn't believe in chairs."

He shrugged. "I married a woman who believes soup deserves ceremony."

"Soup *does* deserve ceremony," she said firmly. "It is a sacred thing."

He watched her ladle carefully, taste, add salt, taste again.
"Well," he admitted, "this is better than what I usually do."

"What do you usually do?"

"Burn it."

She smiled sweetly. "We will be correcting that."

Cottage Two

"So," his wife said, pacing the small room, "you honestly thought women just... *knew* how to sew?"

He winced. "I thought it came with being female."

She dropped into a chair, hands on her knees. "Sir. I learned how to sew because my aunt threw a needle at my head and said, 'Figure it out or go naked.'"

"That seems extreme."

"That was Tuesday."

He grinned. "All right, then teach me."

She raised a brow. "You want to learn to sew?"

"I'd like to know how not to ruin my trousers."

She laughed so hard she had to sit down again. "This marriage is already improving."

Cottage Three

They lay on the floor, heads propped against opposite sides of the hearth.

"You ever been alone this long?" he asked.

She considered. "Alone with someone? No."

"Is it strange?"

She turned her head to look at him. "It's peaceful."

He nodded. "That's the word I've been looking for."

A pause.

"Do you snore?" she asked.

"Only when I'm asleep."

She snorted. "That's usually when it happens."

"Well do you?"

"I sing."

He blinked. "You sing?"

"In my sleep."

"Loudly?"

"Depends on the song."

He smiled. "I suppose we'll learn."

Cottage Four

"Why do you keep apologizing?" she asked.

He froze. "I—what?"

"You've apologized seven times since breakfast. Once for breathing."

"I didn't apologize for breathing."

"You said 'sorry' when you sneezed."

"That was reflex."

She reached over and took his hand. "You don't have to be careful with me."

He swallowed. "I don't know how not to be."

"Then we'll learn together," she said gently. "Marriage isn't a test you pass. It's a conversation you keep having."

He squeezed her hand. "You're very wise."

She smiled. "I learned the hard way."

"Most wisdom is," he said quietly.

Cottage Five

They sat at the table, a map spread between them.

"This is where the creek runs," he said, pointing. "And this ridge gets shade in the afternoon."

She leaned in. "That would be perfect for fruit trees."

"You want fruit trees?"

"I want everything that grows."

He laughed. "You married the right brother."

"Good," she said. "Because I plan to turn this place into something alive."

"It already is."

She looked up at him. "It's about to be more so."

Cottage Six

He stared at her across the bed. "Why are you smiling like that?"

She stretched lazily. "Because no one is knocking on the door."

"No one ever knocks on my door."

"That's because you never stay in one place long enough to have a door."

He chuckled. "Fair."

She sat up. "You know what I learned today?"

"What?"

"That you don't drink coffee."

"I drink it."

"You sip it like it's dangerous."

"It *is* dangerous."

She grinned. "We'll work on that too."

The Second Day

By the second day, laughter echoed from behind closed doors.

184

Arguments happened—but they ended in laughter. Differences surfaced—but curiosity followed. No one pretended to be anything other than what they were.

One wife taught her husband how to dance in the narrow space between bed and table.

"You're stepping on my foot."

"That's because your foot is in my way."

"My foot is where it belongs."

"So is mine."

They collided and fell laughing onto the bed.

Another couple debated prayer styles.

"You pray quietly."

"I listen loudly."

"That doesn't make sense."

"It does to God."

They both paused.

"...Fair enough."

The Third Day

By the third day, time ceased to matter.

Meals were eaten late. Conversations
wandered. Silence became comfortable.
Hands found their way naturally, without fear
or ceremony.

One husband admitted, "I thought marriage
would feel heavier."

"It feels lighter," she agreed.

"That surprises me."

"It shouldn't," she said. "Love doesn't bind. It
frees."

When the couples finally emerged days later—
hair rumpled, eyes bright, steps unhurried—
the ranch felt differently and physically.

Not louder.
Not bigger.

Just **full and fun**.

What one didn't know, the other had taught.
What one feared, the other steadied.
What one lacked, the other supplied.

They had not been hiding.

They had been **becoming one with each other**.

And not one of them regretted a single minute behind those cottage doors.

Chapter 12

The Train That Arrived Too Late

Several days later after the six unexpected marriages and their big marriage celebration event the town got back to its normal activities.

A few days later after its back to normal, the town gathered the way it always did when the rails sang their warning.

Children were pulled close.
Men shaded their eyes.
Women adjusted hats and expectations.

The **bridal train** was coming.

Or so everyone believed.

It arrived midmorning—steam hissing, iron wheels slowing, the conductor stepping down with practiced authority. The crowd leaned forward, eager, curious, already rehearsing their judgments.

But when the doors opened—

Nothing.

No line of hopeful brides.
No nervous laughter.
No gloved hands clutching valises.

Just empty seats.

A murmur rippled through the platform.

"Where are they?"
"Did we miss them?"
"That's not right."

The conductor cleared his throat. "They disembarked earlier. Prior stations."

A gasp.

"All of them?" someone asked.

"Yes, ma'am," he said. "They were already engaged or married by the time we reached the state line."

Silence fell like a dropped plate.

Then six women stepped down.

Not brides.

Missionaries.

They wore dark gray and black—plain dresses cut carefully, hems modest, sleeves long. Their hair was pinned tight, their expressions disciplined. Each carried a Bible and a satchel. They moved in quiet order, as if the world responded best when spoken to firmly.

The crowd shifted.

"Well," someone muttered, disappointed.

The six women surveyed Stillwater Crossing with trained eyes.

This was the town they had been told about.

A place of promise.
A place of order.
A place with *available six pre-designated chosen men* who were unaware of being chosen

They had come to open a **missionary school** for the children—Scripture, hymnody, reading, writing. They had correspondence from local religious women who praised the town's moral fiber and spoke of six Christian brothers of good standing.

Good candidates.

Marriage-minded.

The lead missionary, Miss Eleanor Wright (age thirty, precise, certain), adjusted her gloves.

"This will do," she said.

Her companions nodded.

What none of them knew—what no letter had yet corrected—was that the six men they had been sent to consider were recently married.

Very married.

Across town, the newlywed couples were moving freely, unaware of the incoming collision.

The men were at the **mercantile**, gathering supplies—laughing now, openly, shoulders relaxed. The Stage Six brides were walking Main Street, pausing at vacant buildings, peering through dusty windows, imagining bakeries, sewing rooms, and a dance hall that would make the ground remember joy.

Amy pressed her face to a glass pane. "This would make the *perfect* bakery."

Anne nodded. "Load-bearing walls are sound."

Abby spun once on the boardwalk. "This street needs music."

Asha smiled quietly. "It will have it."

They were mid-laughter when the missionaries approached.

Miss Wright stopped short.

Her eyes moved—quick, assessing.

Married men.
Married women.
Public affection.
Color.

She masked her surprise expertly.

"Good morning," she said coolly. "We are missionaries."

Hannah, who had just arrived with Herbert, smiled warmly. "Welcome."

Miss Wright inclined her head. "We were told this town was... prepared."

Hannah's smile did not waver. "It is."

Her gaze drifted, briefly, to the couples—arms linked, joy unhidden.

Miss Wright followed it.

Her mouth tightened.

The other missionaries exchanged glances.

One whispered, "Those are... the Harvey brothers."

"Yes," another murmured. "All of them."

Miss Wright cleared her throat. "We had expected—"

"I'm sure you did," Hannah said pleasantly.

Miss Wright straightened. "We were sent to assist with moral instruction."

Abby raised an eyebrow. "The children?"

"Yes," Miss Wright said. "And the town."

Amy smiled sweetly. "You're a little late."

That landed.

Miss Wright's voice sharpened. "We were informed these men were available."

Sam stepped forward calmly. "We were. Briefly."

Seth added, smiling now, "God works quickly."

Miss Wright studied the women—makeup, posture, confidence.

"These women," she said carefully, "are… unconventional."

Anne nodded. "That's a polite word."

A missionary whispered, "They dance."

Abby grinned. "Frequently."

Miss Wright folded her hands. "Obedience has a form."

Asha replied softly, "So does faith."

The air tightened.

Hannah stepped in smoothly. "You'll find lodging?"

"Yes," Miss Wright said. "And a place to begin the school."

"Of course," Hannah replied. "The children will learn much."

The missionaries walked on, skirts whispering disapproval.

As they passed, one murmured, "We were told this was a good town."

Hannah heard.

She smiled.

"Oh," she said to Herbert quietly, "it still is."

The couples watched them go.

Abby leaned toward Shane. "They're going to be trouble."

He smiled back, unafraid now. "We're married."

Amy laughed. "And busy."

Anne added, "And building."

The town had expected brides.

Instead, it received **wives**, **missionaries**, and a reckoning.

And Stillwater Crossing was about to learn the difference between obedience and life.

Correction Has a Voice, and It Sounds Like Certainty

The six missionary women arrived together, as if drawn by a single mind rather than six separate hearts.

They walked in measured step, skirts dark and modest, hems untroubled by dust because they lifted them just enough to avoid it. Their trunks were plain—no ribbons, no color, no indulgence. Each carried a Bible worn thin at the edges, not from affection but from repetition. The pages bore marks—underlines, marginal notes, carefully folded corners— evidence of use that had become habit rather than hunger.

They had not come curious.

They had come **sent**.

Their purpose had been agreed upon long
before their feet touched Stillwater Crossing's
dirt road:
to establish a school for the children
and to become the wives of six brothers whose
names had been spoken often—in prayer, in
correspondence, in quiet confidence.

The arrangement was known.
It had been sanctioned.
It had been orderly.

The men had not been informed well in
advance.

What the letters did not prepare them for—
what no dispatch could have anticipated—was
that the brothers had married.

Not months before.
Not weeks before.
But days.

Dance hall women.

The phrase passed through the missionaries
like a bruise forming beneath the skin.

By the time the truth reached them fully, the
marriages were already sealed—legal, public,
witnessed. The wives moved through town
openly now: organizing markets, discussing

leases, laughing without apology, touching their husbands' arms as if affection were not something to be rationed.

The missionaries did not weep.

Their devastation was quiet.

Contained.

And far more dangerous for it.

"There has been deception," Miss Eleanor Wright said finally, folding her hands.

"Not by God," replied Miss Clara Baines, eyes sharp. "By men."

"And women," added Miss Ruth Calder, lips pressed thin.

They did not say the wives' names.
They did not need to.

The women who had married the brothers were discussed as *categories*.
Influences.
Histories.

Past clung to them like a stain no ceremony could wash away.

"If God permitted these unions," said Miss Lydia Howe quietly, "it was only to expose them."

"Unequally yoked," Miss Wright concluded, the phrase falling like a gavel.

The matter, to them, was settled.

They did not speak of reconciliation.
They spoke of **correction**.

The next morning, they moved with intention.

They sought the religious women first—the ones who led prayer circles, taught Sunday lessons, and prided themselves on order. Kitchens and parlors became soft battlegrounds.

They did not accuse.

They *suggested*.

"We're concerned," one missionary would say gently.
"For the children," another added.
"For appearances," a third murmured.
"For influence."

Fear did the rest.

By afternoon, children repeated phrases they barely understood.

Young girls were warned about bright skirts
and music.
Young men cautioned against admiration
mistaken for temptation.

No names were spoken.

Everyone knew who was meant.

Chapter 13

The small room above the church annex smelled of lamp oil and ironed cotton. It had two narrow windows, both shut, and a single table that looked like it had served a hundred meetings where decisions were made without laughter. Six trunks sat in a neat row against the wall, plain as their owners, and the missionaries themselves moved with the same careful efficiency—skirts smoothed, collars straightened, hair checked twice.

Miss Eleanor Wright set the lamp lower so the flame would not waver. She did it with the same calm she used for prayer meetings and reprimands.

"Sit," she said.

They sat. Not slumped. Not sprawled. Six backs straight, six pairs of hands folded or clasped, six faces trained to appear gentle even when they were sharp.

Clara Baines spoke first, voice quiet and quick. "I saw them."

Ruth Calder's mouth tightened. "We all saw them."

Lydia Howe glanced toward the window as if Stillwater itself might be listening. "They were laughing in public."

Eleanor waited until the room settled into silence. Then she folded her hands as if she were beginning a devotion.

"There has been deception," she said.

The word dropped into the room and stayed there.

Clara's eyes narrowed. "Not by God."

Ruth added, lips thin, "By men."

"And women," said Lydia, almost as if she regretted the softness of her own voice and had to harden it by saying more.

No one said the wives' names. They didn't need to. The wives had become something else already—categories. Ideas. Warnings.

Clara leaned forward. "I asked Mrs. Halford at the station if the bridal train had been delayed. She looked at me like I was foolish and said, 'Those Harveys married the dancers last week.'"

Ruth's jaw worked. "Dancers."

Eleanor's expression remained composed, though the muscle near her mouth tightened once. "Our letters were clear."

"Yes," Clara said. "The men were not informed. We were informed."

Lydia's brows pinched. "So how does this marrying dancers happen?"

Ruth answered coldly. "Weakness."

Eleanor lifted her eyes. "Influence."

Clara nodded. "Sensuality disguised as cheer."

Lydia whispered, "And haste."

Ruth drew a breath through her nose. "Dance hall women."

The phrase landed like a verdict. Each woman sat a little straighter, as if the very air of the room required discipline.

Eleanor spoke with careful certainty. "We must not respond with emotion."

Clara's voice sharpened. "This is not emotion. This is order."

Ruth added, "This is duty."

Lydia looked down at her Bible, fingers resting on the worn leather. "What if the Lord permitted it?"

Clara answered too quickly. "He did not permit sin."

Lydia blinked. "I didn't say sin. I said permitted."

Eleanor tilted her head slightly, acknowledging Lydia's carefulness while keeping the room under control. "If God permitted these unions," she said, measured, "it was only to expose them."

Ruth nodded as if she had been waiting for that sentence. "To reveal what was already in those men."

Clara's eyes flashed. "We are not here to despair. We are here to correct."

Eleanor's voice grew firm, the tone that turned Bible lessons into law. "Unequally yoked."

She did not raise her voice. She did not need to.

Lydia swallowed. "But they are legally married."

Clara's gaze cut to her. "Legal does not mean holy."

Ruth added quietly, "And holy does not always look like paper."

Lydia hesitated. "Marriage is still a covenant."

Eleanor's eyes softened just enough to appear merciful. "Covenant requires alignment."

Clara nodded. "And repentance."

Ruth's hands tightened in her lap. "Repentance is not a feeling. It is an action."

Eleanor turned her palms upward slightly, as if she were laying out a lesson plan. "Step by step."

The phrase steadied them. It made anything feel righteous.

Eleanor continued. "First, we establish the school. The children must have structure. That is our official assignment."

Clara added, "And it gives us standing."

Ruth nodded. "Access."

Lydia frowned, uneasy. "Access to what?"

Clara's voice stayed sweet but sharpened at the edges. "To hearts. To homes. To influence."

Eleanor looked at Lydia with mild correction. "We cannot correct what we cannot reach."

Lydia lowered her gaze. "Yes, Miss Wright."

Eleanor continued. "Second, we speak with the religious women. Quietly. Respectfully. We do not accuse. We express concern."

Ruth's mouth curved slightly. "Concern travels faster than accusation."

Clara gave a brief nod. "Fear does the work for you."

Lydia's shoulders tensed. "Is fear... our tool?"

Eleanor answered gently, "Discernment is our tool. Fear is simply what rises when discernment is ignored."

Ruth said, almost pleasantly, "People protect what they fear losing."

Clara added, "We will guide them toward proper protection."

Eleanor's eyes moved from face to face. "Third, we request private conversations gradually with the brothers."

Ruth lifted her chin. "One by one."

Clara's eyes gleamed. "Always calm. Always respectful."

Lydia swallowed again. "And the wives?"

Ruth answered immediately. "We do not address them."

Clara nodded. "Not directly. It gives them power."

Eleanor's tone remained even. "We speak to the men. The men are the gate."

Lydia's voice was barely audible. "But the women are their wives."

Clara smiled the way a teacher smiles when a child asks a question with the wrong assumptions. "Not in spirit, Lydia."

Ruth murmured, "Not in fruit."

Eleanor concluded, "We will ask the question that forces the conscience to speak."

Clara spoke it aloud, soft as a lullaby. "Are you certain this marriage strengthens your walk with God?"

The question hung in the lamplight like a hook. Nobody answered that question.

Ruth nodded once. "And we will remind them that forgiveness is not permission."

Clara added, "Forgiveness does not erase consequences."

Lydia's eyes flickered. "But forgiveness is complete in Christ."

Eleanor answered without shifting her posture. "Salvation is complete. Sanctification requires obedience."

Ruth finished, "Obedience sometimes requires separation."

No one said the word divorce yet. They didn't have to. The idea sat at the center of the table like a covered dish no one would admit they had brought.

Eleanor lowered her gaze to her Bible, then back up. "We will pray. Then we will sleep. Then we will begin."

They prayed with quiet intensity, each woman taking a turn, words stitched with Scripture and certainty. When they rose from their knees, their faces were calm again.

The next morning, they moved with a plan.

They went first to the women who led the town's prayer circles. The ones who hosted Sunday dinners. The ones who measured holiness by hemline and whisper.

In Mrs. Halford's kitchen, Eleanor smiled warmly while accepting a cup of weak tea.

"We're grateful to be here," Eleanor said.

Mrs. Halford clasped her hands. "We're grateful you came. We've had... developments."

Clara tilted her head. "We heard."

Mrs. Halford's mouth tightened. "It was sudden."

Ruth leaned in gently. "We are concerned."

Mrs. Halford's eyes widened. "Concerned?"

"For the children," Ruth said softly.

Mrs. Halford let out a small gasp. "Yes. Exactly."

Clara's voice was sweet as honey. "For appearances."

Mrs. Halford nodded quickly. "Yes."

Eleanor added, "For influence."

Mrs. Halford lowered her voice. "They're bold, those women. Too bold."

Lydia spoke quietly, almost regretting it. "Boldness can be used for good."

Clara turned to her with a smile that warned. "Boldness without modesty becomes a snare."

Mrs. Halford's face lit with agreement. "A snare, yes."

Ruth sighed as if burdened. "We do not want the young ones confused."

Mrs. Halford leaned closer. "The girls were already talking about boots."

Eleanor's eyes softened in practiced concern. "We will help."

By noon, they had visited three parlors and two kitchens. Everywhere they went, they spoke the same careful sentences.

"We're concerned."
"For the children."
"For appearances."
"For influence."

And the town, hungry for righteous panic, accepted it like bread.

By afternoon, children repeated phrases they barely understood.

A boy ran past the mercantile shouting, "Bright skirts are temptation!"

A girl whispered to her friend, "Mama said music makes your soul loose."

A young man, cheeks flushed, told another, "If you look too long, you'll burn."

The wives heard it.

Not first from adults.

From children.

Amy stopped outside a storefront she had been measuring with her eyes. Two little girls passed, holding hands. One pointed at Amy's dress and whispered loudly, "That's the kind of woman the Reverend warned about."

Amy froze.

Abby's jaw tightened. "Did you hear that?"

Anne's eyes went cold. "Yes."

Asha closed her eyes. "Lord, cover their mouths."

Ada said softly, "They're teaching fear."

Across town, the missionaries began the private conversations.

They did not start with the youngest. They started with the eldest.

Sam Harvey after being summoned by the religious women of the town on an urgent matter that they claimed. There he met and received Eleanor in the parlor of the church with the other religious women of the town, hat in his hands, posture upright. He was polite because he had been raised to be. His jaw was tight because he was a man learning new boundaries.

Eleanor smiled warmly. "Mr. Harvey. You have quite a reputation."

Sam nodded once. "Thank you, ma'am."

"You've been faithful," she continued.

"I try."

"You're disciplined."

He said nothing.

"You have such potential," she finished gently, as if offering him a gift.

Sam's eyes narrowed slightly. "What is it you want to say, Miss Wright?"

Eleanor's smile did not falter. "Only to ask— are you certain this marriage strengthens your walk with God?"

Sam's fingers tightened on his hat.

"My marriage is my responsibility," he said, voice steady.

Eleanor's tone remained soft. "Responsibility and blessing are not always the same."

Sam held her gaze. "Ada strengthens me."

Eleanor blinked once. "Does she?"

"She does," Sam repeated.

Eleanor sighed as if pained. "Mr. Harvey... obedience sometimes feels like loss."

Sam's voice lowered. "And sometimes control feels like holiness."

Eleanor's eyes sharpened for a breath. "Be careful."

Sam rose. "I'm being careful now."

The next conversation was Seth.

Clara met him near the church steps, after he had deposited his wife and was settling the horse and wagon before church. She appeared to be speaking as if she were offering counsel to a brother.

"You know Scripture well," she said.

Seth nodded. "Yes, ma'am."

"And grace?" Clara asked gently.

Seth's mouth tightened. "I'm learning."

Clara smiled. "Learning requires correction."

Seth stared at her. "My wife is not an assignment."

Clara's voice stayed calm. "Is she strengthening your walk with God?"

Seth laughed once, sharp. "She is feeding the poor, praying out loud, and making bread that could raise the dead."

Clara's brow lifted. "Bread is not holiness."

Seth leaned closer. "But fruit is."

Clara stepped back slightly, still composed. "You will be tested."

Seth nodded. "We already are."

After church while going for the wagon to bring his wife home, Silas ran into Ruth, and the conversation was almost silent.

Ruth spoke softly. "You are a quiet man."

Silas nodded.

"Quiet men often listen best," Ruth continued. "Tell me... are you certain this marriage strengthens your walk with God?"

Silas looked at her for a long time.

Then he spoke, barely above a whisper. "Asha prays more than anyone I've ever met."

Ruth's lips tightened. "Prayer can be counterfeit."

Silas's eyes lifted. "Not hers."

Ruth tried again, gentler. "Sometimes the Lord removes what distracts."

Silas answered calmly, "Sometimes the Lord sends what heals."

Saul met Lydia one day going into the mercantile to pick up items for his household She bristled from the beginning.

When Lydia approached him with her gentle face and careful words, he didn't wait for the question.

"You came for us? we heard" he said.

Lydia blinked. "We came for the children."

Saul's mouth curved bitterly. "And the Harvey brothers."

Lydia lowered her voice. "Are you certain this marriage—"

Saul cut her off. "I am certain my wife sees things I refuse to see. That is why I married her."

Lydia's cheeks flushed. "You're being defensive."

Saul's eyes hardened. "I'm being married."

Scott grew restless when Clara tried to charm him with compliments in front of the post office in town .

"You've been obedient," she said.

Scott answered, "I've been quiet."

Clara's smile stayed. "Quietness is a virtue."

Scott shook his head. "Quietness can be fear."

Clara's eyes narrowed. "Are you certain this marriage strengthens your walk with God?"

Scott laughed, restless and real. "I'm certain I can breathe now."

Clara's voice turned slightly sharper. "Breathing is not doctrine."

Scott leaned in. "But life is."

Shane burned.

When Eleanor approached him outside the bank one day, he didn't wait. He spoke first.

"You're late," he said.

Eleanor blinked. "Excuse me?"

"You're late," Shane repeated, voice shaking with contained heat. "You were coming to claim us like prizes. You were late."

Eleanor's eyes cooled. "We came under instruction."

Shane nodded. "And we married under mercy."

Eleanor's voice softened again, dangerous in its gentleness. "Are you certain this marriage strengthens your walk with God?"

Shane stepped closer. "Yes."

Eleanor's brows lifted. "So certain."

Shane's voice broke just slightly. "Because God likes her. And I didn't know He could like women like her until He gave her to me."

Eleanor's face flickered—something like contempt disguised as sorrow. "You are young."

Shane smiled, fierce. "And married."

By the time the town realized what was happening, lines had already been drawn.

Not between righteousness and sin.

Between control and fruit.
Between law and covenant.
Between appearance and transformation.

The Stage Six noticed the change first.

It came in glances withdrawn.

When Abby entered the mercantile, conversation stopped. A woman turned her face away as if Abby's perfume could stain her.

When Amy spoke to a child, the child stared down at her shoes and whispered, "Mama said we shouldn't talk to you too long."

When Ana offered bread to a neighbor, the neighbor accepted it quickly but avoided her eyes, as if gratitude might be mistaken for agreement.

Anne counted it like inventory. "those missionaries are isolating us and dividing us between the town folks."

Abby nodded. "Teaching fear."

"Systematically," Anne added, voice flat.

Asha closed her eyes. "And they believe it is love."

Ada's voice was quiet, dignified. "It is control."

Hannah watched it all without rushing.

She moved through the town with her chin lifted, smile intact, eyes sharp.

She had seen this kind of righteousness before. Righteousness that used Scripture like a rope. Righteousness that corrected what it did not understand. Righteousness that called fruit dangerous because it didn't grow in the approved garden.

She did not panic.

She waited.

Because correction that believes itself holy always overreaches.

And when it does, truth does not need to shout.

It stands.

It feeds.

It heals.

It dances.

And Stillwater Crossing—caught between two visions of faith—was about to find out which one could actually give life.

The door was once again shut firmly this time, the latch set, the curtains drawn. Morning light tried to push through the fabric, but it was muted, filtered, disciplined—much like the women inside.

Miss Eleanor Wright stood at the center reiterating the past events and circumstances. She wanted desperately to marry a Harvey brother at all cost. The more they saw them and how they treated their wives the missionaries got more jealous and deceptive.

Her Bible lay open on the table, not as something to read, but as something to **authorize** what was already decided.

"This is no longer confusion," Eleanor said quietly. "It is opportunity."

Clara Baines nodded at once. "They married quickly."

"Too quickly," Ruth Calder added. "That alone proves influence."

Lydia Howe hesitated. "Or certainty."

Clara's eyes snapped toward her. "Certainty does not arrive with laughter and color."

Eleanor lifted one finger, not sharply, but decisively. "We must be precise. These men are not rebels."

"No," Ruth agreed. "They are *pliable*."

"They were raised right," Clara said. "That is what makes this salvageable."

Lydia folded her hands tightly. "But they are already married."

Eleanor met her gaze steadily. "Marriage is not a spell."

Silence followed that.

Then Ruth spoke, voice low and careful. "What God joins together—"

Eleanor interrupted without raising her voice. "—presumes God was the one joining."

Clara leaned forward. "Improper influence disqualifies consent."

Lydia's throat tightened. "You're saying the vows don't count."

"I'm saying," Eleanor replied evenly, "that God does not ratify disorder."

Ruth nodded. "If He allowed it, it was to reveal it."

Lydia whispered, "That is dangerous reasoning."

Eleanor's eyes sharpened. "So is sentimentality."

Clara exhaled. "We are not talking about cruelty. We are talking about correction."

"Yes," Ruth said. "Guidance."

"Redirection," Eleanor finished.

Lydia pressed her lips together. "At whatever cost?"

Eleanor's reply was immediate. "At the cost of obedience."

That ended the debate.

They continued to plan.

Step by step.

Quietly.

Clara tapped the table. "We do not confront the wives."

"Never," Ruth said. "That gives them legitimacy."

Eleanor nodded. "We deal with the men. They are the hinge."

Lydia frowned. "And Hannah Harvey, their mother and mother-inlaw?"

Eleanor smiled thinly. "She believes she has won."

Clara added, "Which makes her careless."

Ruth said, "We let her talk."

Eleanor continued, voice calm and instructional. "Scripture is not used to explain. It is used to **frame**."

"Fragments," Clara said approvingly.

"Yes," Eleanor replied. "Full passages invite argument."

Ruth smiled faintly. "Fragments invite submission."

Lydia shifted in her chair. "What about covenant?"

Clara responded briskly. "Covenant requires holiness."

"And holiness," Ruth added, "requires order."

Eleanor concluded, "Order requires leadership."

They all nodded.

That afternoon, Eleanor approached Sam Harvey outside the mercantile.

"Mr. Harvey," she said pleasantly.

Sam inclined his head. "Miss Wright."

She walked beside him, not too close, not distant. Perfectly measured.

"You've been busy," she said.

"Yes, ma'am."

"Providing," she added. "A godly trait."

Sam said nothing.

Eleanor continued, "Men like you are rare. Steady. Dependable. Worth preserving."

Sam's jaw tightened. "Preserving from what?"

She smiled gently. "From distraction."

He stopped walking.

"My wife is not a distraction."

Eleanor's tone softened. "Of course not intentionally. But intention does not negate effect."

Sam's voice was controlled. "Ada strengthens me."

224

Eleanor tilted her head. "Does she strengthen your *discipline*?"

Sam stared at her. "She strengthens my peace."

Eleanor nodded slowly, as if conceding something small. "Peace can be deceptive."

He folded his arms. "So can control."

Her smile did not change. "Have you prayed about separation?"

Sam stiffened. "Separation from my wife?"

"For clarity," Eleanor said smoothly. "For prayer."

"No," Sam said firmly.

Eleanor lowered her voice. "Would you be willing to fast?"

Sam paused.

"Yes," he said carefully. "Together with my wife."

Eleanor blinked. "Together?"

"With my wife," Sam finished.

That conversation ended abruptly.

Clara met on another occasion, Seth near the church steps.

"You look tired," she observed.

Seth laughed lightly. "Marriage will do that, but in a awesome fun and loving way."

Clara smiled. "Marriage should energize holiness."

Seth looked at her. "It energizes life and love."

Clara stepped closer. "Life without discipline becomes indulgence."

Seth crossed his arms. "Are you accusing my wife?"

"I'm protecting your soul," Clara replied.

"By questioning my joy?"

"By testing it," she said softly. "True joy survives scrutiny."

Seth leaned in. "Then test yours."

Clara stiffened. "This isn't about me."

"It never is, you all came here to marry Harvey men but it's too late" Seth said, and walked away.

Ruth approached Silas in the evening, near the fence line.

"You are a man of few words," she said kindly.

Silas nodded.

"That often means depth," Ruth continued. "But depth must be guided."

Silas looked at her calmly. "Asha guides me well."

Ruth smiled thinly. "She is... quiet."

"She listens," Silas replied.

"Listening without correction can be dangerous," Ruth said.

Silas shook his head slowly. "Correction without love is violence."

Ruth inhaled sharply. "Be careful how you speak of obedience."

Silas met her eyes. "Be careful how you speak of marriage."

Saul did not wait for his turn.

He found Lydia near the schoolhouse.

"You want to talk to me," he said bluntly.

Lydia startled. "I—yes."

He folded his arms. "Say it."

She swallowed. "Are you certain this marriage—"

"—strengthens my walk with God?" Saul finished. "Yes."

Lydia frowned. "You answered too quickly."

Saul shrugged. "Because I know the difference between guilt and conviction."

She whispered, "Sometimes guilt is conviction."

He stepped closer. "And sometimes it's manipulation, like trying to marry men who are already married"

Lydia stepped back, shaken.

Scott laughed outright when Clara approached him again.

"You're relentless," he said.

"We are faithful," Clara replied.

"To what, trying to breakup marriages?" he asked.

"To order."

Scott nodded slowly. "That explains why you're so uncomfortable with joy."

Shane was the last.

Eleanor sought him out deliberately.

"You are young," she said.

"Yes, ma'am."

"Impressionable."

"Not anymore after being married to my loving wife."

She smiled gently. "God tests young men first."

Shane looked her straight in the eye. "God gave me my wife. Not you"

Eleanor's voice cooled. "God does not rush."

Shane answered quietly, "Neither does love."

Eleanor studied him. "Would you be willing to step away from her if God asked?"

Shane didn't hesitate. "God wouldn't."

Her eyes flashed. "You presume much."

Shane smiled sadly. "So do you."

Behind them, the town shifted.

Children repeated lessons they didn't understand.

"Mama says dancing opens doors."

"Teacher says bright colors invite trouble."

"You shouldn't talk to them too long."

Approval became conditional.

Fellowship selective.

At the edge of town, Abby watched a woman cross the street to avoid her.

"They're isolating us," she said quietly.

Anne nodded. "Incrementally."

Amy's voice shook. "They're trying to starve us socially."

Asha closed her eyes. "This is spiritual violence."

Ada said nothing, but her spine straightened.

Hannah observed it all.

She said nothing.She did nothing.

Yet.

Because she knew something the missionaries did not.

Control always overplays its hand.

And covenant—true covenant—does not dissolve under pressure.

It reveals itself.

And when it does, it exposes everything that tried to replace it.

The missionaries pressed forward—quiet, relentless, convinced that they were going to breakup these marriages and marry the Harvey brothers.

They believed God would honor their resolve.

They did not yet realize they were no longer fighting sin.

They were fighting **fruit**., Fruits of the Spirit, Love

And fruit, once seen, cannot be unseen.

Chapter 14

Religion, for the missionaries, was no longer merely doctrine.
It had become **instrument**.

They met again after dusk.

The same small room. The same tight chairs. The same lamp turned low—not for humility, but for privacy. Outside, Stillwater Crossing settled into evening, unaware that decisions were being sharpened just above the church ceiling.

Miss Eleanor Wright did not sit immediately.

She stood.

That alone silenced the others.

"This is not a tragedy," she said calmly. "It is an opening."

Clara Baines nodded at once. "An exposed seam."

Ruth Calder folded her hands. "A moment that requires direction."

Lydia Howe hesitated. "Or restraint."

Eleanor turned her head slowly. "Restraint is what allowed this disorder."

The word landed cleanly.

"The men are not rebels," Clara continued. "That's the key."

"No," Ruth agreed. "Rebels resist. These men complied."

"With *who*," Lydia asked softly.

"With influence," Eleanor answered. "Which can be replaced."

She finally sat.

"What matters," Eleanor said, voice measured, "is not consent."

Clara leaned forward. "It is outcome."

Lydia's breath caught. "Consent matters."

Eleanor's eyes lifted. "Consent is shaped by understanding. And understanding can be corrected."

No one spoke for a moment.

Then Ruth said, "We must be very clear among ourselves."

"Yes," Eleanor agreed. "Speak plainly."

Ruth continued, "Those marriages cannot be God-joined."

Clara added immediately, "Not formed under improper influence."

Lydia whispered, "They stood before a minister."

Clara replied sharply, "Ceremony does not sanctify confusion."

Eleanor nodded. "Marriage requires more than words. It requires alignment."

"With whom?" Lydia asked.

"With God," Eleanor replied smoothly.

"And with us, we want to marry these men and get the full benefits of the love that they are giving to their wives." Clara said without flinching.

That settled it.

Eleanor opened her Bible—not to read, but to point.

"People misuse this verse," she said, tapping the page. "'What God has joined together, let no man divide.'"

Clara scoffed quietly. "Assumes God did the joining."

"Exactly," Eleanor said. "If God was not the author, then man is not dividing—he is correcting."

Lydia's voice trembled. "That is a dangerous claim."

Eleanor met her gaze. "So is allowing corruption to masquerade as covenant."

Ruth exhaled slowly. "We are not speaking of force."

"No," Clara said. "Never force."

Eleanor's lips curved faintly. "We are speaking of **guidance**."

They began outlining methods like teachers preparing a syllabus.

"We never say divorce," Clara said.

"Never," Ruth agreed.

"We say reflection," Eleanor added.

"Prayer," Clara said.

"Distance," Ruth finished.

Lydia looked between them. "Distance from their wives."

"For clarity," Eleanor said gently.

"For discernment," Clara added.

"For obedience," Ruth concluded.

Each phrase sounded harmless alone.

Together, they formed a wedge.

"Scripture must be applied selectively," Clara said matter-of-factly.

"Fragments," Eleanor agreed. "Full passages invite resistance."

Ruth smiled thinly. "Fragments invite submission."

Lydia whispered, "That's manipulation."

Eleanor replied without heat, "That's leadership."

They reviewed verses aloud—not reading them fully, but trimming them.

"'Obedience is better than sacrifice,'" Clara quoted.

"Without mentioning context," Ruth said approvingly.

"'Flee youthful lusts,'" Eleanor added.

"Define lust loosely," Clara said.

"'Be ye separate,'" Ruth continued.

"And never clarify from what," Eleanor finished.

Lydia stood abruptly. "You are weaponizing Scripture."

Eleanor remained seated. "Scripture has always been a sword."

"A sword can cut the wrong person," Lydia said.

"And a surgeon's knife looks violent to the untrained," Clara replied.

Silence followed.

Then Eleanor spoke quietly. "If Lydia cannot assist, she may observe."

Lydia sank back into her chair.

They moved on.

"Next," Eleanor said, "we gather support."

"Letters are already drafted," Ruth said, pulling folded pages from her bag. "Back east."

Clara smiled. "Moral emergency."

"Yes," Ruth confirmed. "No accusations. Only concern."

Eleanor nodded. "Language matters."

"What about the local leaders?" Clara asked.

"I've spoken with two elders already," Ruth said. "They're uneasy."

"Unease is fertile ground," Eleanor said.

"And the women?" Clara asked.

Eleanor smiled faintly. "They are the backbone."

"Invite them," Ruth said.

"Privately," Clara added.

"With tea," Eleanor finished. "Always tea."

Lydia whispered, "And fear."

Eleanor corrected gently, "Protection."

"Children first," Ruth said. "Always the children."

Clara nodded. "They repeat what they're taught."

"And repetition creates reality," Eleanor said.

They paused.

Then Clara asked, "What if the men resist?"

Eleanor folded her hands. "Then we praise their faith."

"And question their judgment," Ruth added.

"And isolate," Clara said quietly.

Lydia's head snapped up. "Isolate?"

Eleanor's voice remained smooth. "Selective fellowship."

Ruth explained, "Church roles reconsidered. Invitations delayed. Opportunities withheld."

"Until?" Lydia asked.

"Until clarity emerges and it is clearly understood that we are the real wives of the Harvey brothers," Eleanor said.

"And if the wives confront us?" Clara asked.

"They won't," Eleanor replied. "We never address them directly."

"Why?" Lydia demanded.

"Because confronting them would require acknowledging them," Ruth said.

"And acknowledgment creates legitimacy," Clara added.

Eleanor leaned forward. "We are not dismantling women."

"We are dismantling influence."

The next day, the work began once again in earnest haste.

In a kitchen near the edge of town, Eleanor spoke softly to a group of women.

"We're worried," she said.

"About the children," Ruth added.

"And about example," Clara murmured.

One woman whispered, "They laugh too much."

Another said, "My daughter asked about dancing."

Eleanor sighed. "That is how it starts."

In the schoolroom, Ruth corrected a lesson.

"Order," she said firmly. "Order reflects holiness."

A child repeated it.

In the churchyard, Clara spoke to a group of young men.

"Association carries weight," she warned.

One nodded. Another looked uncertain.

By evening, whispers had become currents.

That night, Eleanor met again with the missionaries.

"They're responding," Clara said.

Ruth smiled. "Good."

"And the men?" Eleanor asked.

"They're unsettled," Ruth replied. "That's enough."

Lydia finally spoke. "You are breaking something alive."

Eleanor looked at her evenly. "Sometimes a bone must be broken to reset."

"What if it heals wrong?" Lydia asked.

Eleanor stood. "Then it was never sound."

241

They prayed.

Not for wisdom.

For success.

And as they bowed their heads, convinced of victory, the marriages they sought to dismantle continued to stand—not because they were perfect, but because they were **real**.

Tested not by worldliness.

But by religion itself.

The wives saw it long before the town named it.

"They're hungry," Abby said quietly, watching the way the missionaries crossed the street together, skirts brushing in perfect order.

"Hunger pretending to be discipline," Anne replied. "That's the most dangerous kind."

Ada folded her hands in her lap. "They're not looking at the fruit. They're looking at control."

Ana shook her head slowly. "They keep saying holiness, but nothing about it feels like love."

Asha spoke softly, eyes closed. "Because it isn't."

They sat together, not huddled, not fearful—just attentive.

"They think we don't know Scripture," Amy said, a humorless laugh escaping her. "As if joy disqualifies us from reading."

Abby leaned back. "They quote pieces. Never the whole."

Ada nodded. "Pieces don't require obedience. Only agreement."

Ana sighed. "Jesus never spoke in fragments."

Asha opened her eyes. "He spoke plainly."

They were quiet a moment.

"I know Him," Abby said. "Not as a threat. Not as a ruler in the corner watching hems and smiles."

"I know Him as love," Amy said. "As bread shared, not withheld."

Ada's voice was steady. "Love one another. That was not a suggestion."

Anne added, "Love your neighbor as yourself. No footnotes."

Ana smiled sadly. "They don't want love. They want alignment."

"They don't believe covenant is sacred," Abby said. "Only useful."

Asha whispered, "They believe marriage can be revised, the bottom line is that they want our husbands for themselves, they are jealous of our relationships and outwardly showing affection."

Silence followed.

Then Amy said, "We are not unequally yoked."

"No," Ada agreed. "We walk the same direction."

Anne crossed her arms. "They're trying to make obedience cruel."

Ana shook her head. "Obedience never asked me to destroy."

Abby leaned forward. "What they call discernment is ambition."

"And resentment," Anne added.

They all felt it now—the thing no one had named out loud yet.

"They look at our husbands like property, their property" Amy said finally.

Ada's jaw tightened. "Not with affection."

"Not with warmth," Abby said.

"With ownership," Anne finished.

Ana's voice dropped. "They admire without loving."

Asha said quietly, "They desire without tenderness."

Abby scoffed. "Self-denial worn like armor."

"And pride like skin," Anne added.

Amy frowned. "They think severity is virtue."

Ada's eyes followed the missionaries again. "They don't know how to love men like ours."

Ana tilted her head. "Men who listen."

"Men who work," Abby said.

"Men who don't dominate," Anne added.

"But partner," Asha finished.

Amy nodded. "That kind of man always draws attention."

"And resentment," Ada said.

Abby exhaled. "Especially from people who believe they earned righteousness."

Anne's voice sharpened. "They hate diversity."

Ana smiled faintly. "Because it cannot be arranged."

Asha said softly, "They are afraid of what they cannot order."

"And women who don't ask permission," Abby added.

That night, behind closed doors, the wives gathered.

Not to argue.

Not to panic.

Not to accuse.

"We pray," Ada said simply.

Ana nodded. "For clarity."

Amy added, "For wisdom."

Asha said, "For unity."

Abby looked around the room. "Not for their downfall."

Anne shook her head. "No."

"For truth," Ada said.

They knelt.

Not dramatically.

Not loudly.

Just honestly.

"This is a test," Ana said afterward, wiping her eyes. "Too soon."

Amy nodded. "The joy hasn't even settled yet."

"And already the storm," Abby murmured.

Asha closed her eyes. "The enemy never announces himself."

"He arrives dressed like righteousness," Anne said.

"Offering counsel," Ada added.

"Promising peace," Ana said.

"At the cost of separation," Abby finished.

They spoke collectively to their husbands that same night.

No tears.

No ultimatums.

No performance.

"We chose each other," Ada said to Sam. "And I still choose you."

Sam swallowed. "I choose you too."

Ana held Seth's hands. "Remember how we prayed before the train stopped."

Seth nodded. "I haven't forgotten."

Asha said quietly to Silas, "Our peace is not counterfeit."

Silas squeezed her fingers. "I know."

Anne looked Saul in the eye. "I won't compete."

Saul shook his head. "You never had to."

Amy laughed softly with Scott. "Truth doesn't need volume."

Scott smiled. "And neither do you."

Abby leaned into Shane. "We don't need to prove anything."

Shane kissed her forehead. "We just need to stand."

Meanwhile, the missionaries escalated.

"They're confused," Clara said to a visiting elder.

"They're under influence," Eleanor told a prayer circle.

"The wives are temporary," Ruth whispered to a matron.

"Divorce would be deliverance," someone said aloud for the first time.

Behind closed doors, the missionaries nodded.

"We're winning," Clara said.

"Cost doesn't matter," Ruth agreed.

"Righteousness demands sacrifice," Eleanor concluded.

They told themselves broken homes were acceptable.

That love could be postponed.

That devastation was evidence of truth working.

What they did not see—

What they refused to see—

Was that the marriages they sought to dismantle were strengthening?

Quietly.

Steadily.

Anchored.

Covenant does not shout.

It holds.

And as the pressure increased, the wives stood.

Not defiant.

Not loud.

But discerning.

Watchful.

Unmoving.

Knowing this would not be won by argument.

Only by truth—revealed in time.

Chapter 15

The wives began to see the confusion plainly, because it no longer bothered to hide itself.

"They're not circling anymore," Abby said, her voice low as she set down a crate of produce. "They're advancing."

Anne wiped her hands on her apron and glanced toward the fence line where two missionary women stood speaking to a ranch hand. "They've stopped asking permission."

Ada's eyes narrowed. "They don't believe they need it."

Ana watched from the shade of the wagon. "Their concern has teeth now."

Asha spoke softly. "Concern has been replaced with instruction."

The missionary women appeared everywhere—too close, too often. At the edge of the fields. Near the market tables. Along the road where the wives walked together in the mornings.

"You should consider obedience," one missionary said aloud one afternoon, her voice clear enough to carry. "Seasons of separation are biblical."

Abby stopped walking. "Separation from what?"

"From confusion," the woman replied smoothly. "From emotion."

Anne stepped forward. "From wives?"

The missionary did not blink. "From influence."

That was when the tone changed.

"It would be best," another missionary said later, folding her hands, "for the brothers to move back into the family home. Just for a time."

"A season," one added quickly. "Not rejection."

"Obedience," said a third.

Ana felt her chest tighten. "And where would you be?"

"With them," came the calm reply. "For prayer."

Asha's voice was quiet but steady. "In our absence?."

"Yes," the missionary answered without hesitation. "Without distraction."

They spoke of supper shared in order. Scripture discussed freely. Men strengthened without interruption.

Harmless, they called it.

"Even seating at church can help," one suggested brightly. "Men beside us. Wives apart."

Abby laughed once, sharp. "You call that unity?"

"Spiritual clarity," the woman replied.

Ada said nothing then. She was watching the men.

A season

The brothers were shaken. They were tired. They needed peace from this division.

Sam rubbed his temples late one night. "Every voice says something different."

Seth stared at the floor. "I don't know how peace can feel so... contested."

Silas spoke slowly. "They say distance clarifies."

Saul exhaled. "They say obedience requires sacrifice."

Scott paced. "What if stepping back helps us hear God?"

Shane swallowed. "What if it's just for a season?"

They convinced themselves with care.

"It's not rejection," Sam said.

"It's discipline," Seth added.

"It's quiet," Silas offered.

"It's seeking God," Saul concluded.

When they brought the idea to their wives, their voices were careful. Ashamed.

"We thought," Sam said to Ada, "maybe a little distance."

Ada nodded once. "I hear you."

Seth couldn't meet Ana's eyes. "Just for clarity."

Ana reached for his hand. "I understand what you're being told."

Silas whispered, "It doesn't change how I feel."

Asha smiled gently. "I know."

Not one wife argued.

Not one pleaded.

Abby listened to Shane, then said simply, "I won't fight you."

Anne looked at Saul. "But I won't pretend this is neutral."

Amy touched Scott's arm. "You're confused. I'm not."

The wives were clear, by the next day they knew what they were going to do.

"This is isolation," Anne said later, once they were alone. "Step one."

"Access," Abby added. "Step two."

"Influence," Ada finished.

Ana nodded. "And then replacement."

Asha closed her eyes. "Separation is never neutral."

They chose movement.

They prepared quietly.

"We still have funds," Anne said, opening the ledger.

"We still have unity," Abby replied.

"We still have vision," Ada said.

When the men moved back into the main house after the following day, the wives did not collapse inward.

They hitched two wagons themselves.

"Town," Abby said. "Now."

They drove straight to the land office.

"One acre each," Anne told the clerk, calm and direct. "Within town limits."

He blinked. "That's unusual."

"So are we," Abby replied.

They purchased two abandoned storefronts and an old bakery and a boardinghouse no one else wanted.

"Prices are low," the clerk said suspiciously.

Ana smiled. "We noticed."

Every deed was signed carefully.

One name.

The Stage Six.

They walked the bakery together.

"The ovens are sound," Amy said, running her hand along the brick.

"Waiting," Abby said.

They hired local men.

"Can you rebuild?" Anne asked.

"Yes," the man replied. "No questions."

"Good," she said.

Walls were scrubbed. Floors repaired. Windows reopened.

Asha prayed quietly over the space. "Let this feed many."

Nearby, they moved into the once abandoned boardinghouse.

"Close enough to walk," Ada said.

"Close enough to build," Abby agreed.

They moved in together.

Not desperate.

Focused.

At night, the ache came.

"I miss him," Amy admitted.

"Yes," Ana said softly. "That part is real."

"But despair doesn't belong here," Ada replied.

They believed truth would expose itself.

In the meantime, they built.

"A market," Abby said, sketching in the dirt.

"An amphitheater," Anne added. "Small."

"For families," Ana said.

"For daylight," Asha whispered.

Something unexpected happened.

They laughed again.

Not recklessly.

Steadily.

"This feels right," Amy said one morning, watching the sun hit the open windows.

"We're creating," Abby replied.

"While others whisper," Anne said.

They did not know how long the test would last.

But they knew this:

They would not wait in stillness.

They would not shrink.

They would build.

Until clarity returned.

Until deception collapsed.

Until what was planted in love stood visible to all.

Chapter 16

Something changed at the Harvey Ranch.

It did not arrive like thunder.
It came softly, repeatedly, the way erosion works—grain by grain, Sunday after Sunday, dressed in certainty.

"They're coming again," Scott said one afternoon, standing near the window as six figures approached from the road.

Sam did not answer right away. "They always do."

The missionary women arrived together, never separately, never late, never early. Always together. Always certain. They did not knock. They were never invited. And yet, no one stopped them.

They carried dinner.

Heavy pots. Covered dishes. Set down with solemn care, as though the act itself were worship.

"This is for the family," Eleanor said calmly, already moving toward the table.

The men were directed without words.

"Sit," Clara said, gesturing.

"Wait," Ruth added.

No one was asked to help.

No one was invited into the work of it.

The food was placed before them—gray, heavy, lifeless. Potatoes boiled too long. Meat without seasoning. Bread dense and dry. It filled the stomach but starved the spirit.

Seth swallowed and forced a nod. "Thank you."

Eleanor inclined her head. "It's important to keep things simple."

They did not eat much themselves.

They moved stiffly through the house, skirts brushing furniture as if marking territory. Their voices stayed low, controlled. No laughter. No teasing. No memory shared.

This was not fellowship.

This was occupation.

When the meal ended, they cleared the table themselves. Not as service. As signal.

"This is how it should be," Clara said softly, stacking plates. "Order."

"Quiet," Ruth added.

"Submission," Eleanor finished.

They called it godliness.

"Jesus lived plainly," Eleanor said later, standing near the hearth. "Restraint is holiness."

"Emotion opens doors," Clara warned. "Error enters through feeling."

"Joy is not a fruit to be chased," Ruth said. "It distracts."

Saul felt something twist in his chest. "I thought joy was—"

Eleanor cut him off gently. "Joy follows obedience. Never precedes it."

What they described sounded nothing like love.

But it sounded very much like control.

They mistook the absence of joy for purity and called it righteousness.

Nearly every visit circled back to the same subject.

The wives.

"They are not content to remain in their place," Clara said one Sunday, voice sharp.

"The bakery is an act of defiance," Ruth added.

"Buying land independently?" Eleanor shook her head. "Manipulation."

"And that amphitheater," Clara said quietly, "corruption in progress."

Seth stiffened. "They're feeding people."

"They're gathering influence," Ruth replied.

"They're proud," Eleanor said calmly. "Dangerously independent."

Everything the wives touched was reframed.

Provision became rebellion.
Creation became threat.
Joy became sin dressed attractively.

The men listened.

At first, politely.

Then uneasily.

Eventually, silently.

After the missionaries left, the house felt wrong.

Prayer no longer settled easily. Scripture felt narrower, as if someone had folded the pages inward. Silence pressed instead of comforted.

"This doesn't feel like conviction," Scott muttered one night. "It feels... heavy."

Silas nodded slowly. "Conviction brings clarity."

"This brings confusion," Shane said.

The missionaries mistook this weariness for progress.

"They're softening," Clara said one evening, satisfied.

"They're yielding," Ruth agreed.

They did not notice the way the men lingered by the windows after supper, staring toward town.

They did not hear how often names were spoken when they were gone.

"Ada would've seasoned this," Sam said once, quietly.

"Ana would've laughed at this bread," Seth murmured another time.

"Asha would've prayed without tightening the room," Silas added.

Months passed.

What the missionaries believed was conquest was erosion.

Not of faith.

But of patience.

Of tolerance.

Of illusion.

The men grew tired.

Not angry.

Tired.

The kind of tired that comes when something drains without giving life back.

They missed their wives.

Not just their presence—but their counsel. Their steadiness. Their laughter. The way faith had once felt wide instead of narrow.

Then the missionaries pressed too far.

One Sunday, after another joyless meal, Eleanor did not soften her voice.

"We need to be clear," she said.

The men looked up.

"God is patient," she continued, "but He does not compromise."

Clara folded her hands. "These unions cannot stand."

Ruth spoke plainly. "You must choose."

Sam felt his heart stop. "Choose what?"

"Dismiss your wives," Eleanor said evenly. "Annul what was done in error."

"And take vows aligned with God's will," Clara added.

Ruth finished it. "Or live under unforgiveness and damnation."

The words landed without mercy.

No prayer followed.

No space.

No gentleness.

Just demand.

The room went quiet.

Not the quiet of submission.

The quiet of recognition.

Something broke in that silence.

Not loudly.

Not dramatically.

But decisively.

Saul felt it first. *This isn't love.*

Seth's jaw tightened. *This isn't God.*

Silas closed his eyes. *This is possession.*

Shane's hands curled into fists. *This is threat.*

For the first time, the words were stripped bare.

Not guidance.

Demand.

Not faith.

Control.

Not love.

Fear.

The missionaries believed they had reached victory.

They did not see what had just happened.

Ultimatums, when spoken in the name of God, expose the heart of the one who gives them.

And the Harvey brothers—tired, tested, and finally awake—were no longer confused about what love was not.

Chapter 17

The Answer Was Already Chosen

The Harvey brothers did not argue with the ultimatum.

They listened.

That alone unsettled the missionaries, though they did not recognize it at the time. There were no raised voices, no defensive postures, no pleading explanations. The brothers stood where they were, hats in hand, shoulders squared, faces unreadable.

Silence stretched.

Then Sam Harvey spoke, his voice level, respectful, and firm.

"Come back next Sunday," he said. "We will have our answer for you then."

The words were neither refusal nor agreement. They were an ending disguised as patience.

The missionaries mistook composure for surrender.

They left the ranch buoyant, nearly light-headed with certainty. Their steps down the drive were quick, purposeful, already moving toward a future they believed had been secured. By the time they reached the road, Clara was smiling openly.

"They know," she said.

"They've yielded," Ruth replied.

Eleanor said nothing, but her confidence showed in her stride. She had seen this before. Men always resisted briefly before conceding to what was framed as righteousness.

By the time they returned to their rented house, the air inside felt celebratory. Trunks were pulled open. Dresses were removed, shaken, folded neatly. Plain colors were arranged carefully, already being matched to imagined ceremonies. Books were stacked by topic. Scripture references were reviewed and underlined again.

"They won't delay long," Clara said, sorting through correspondence paper. "Men like them value order."

"Especially when pressured properly," Ruth added.

Letters were written that night—carefully worded updates sent back east to the mission board. Nothing explicit, nothing reckless. Only progress. Only obedience forming under correction. The phrase moral restoration appeared more than once.

They visited the religious women of the town the following days, speaking in lowered voices, eyes shining with purpose.

"It's happening," Eleanor told them.
"God is moving," Clara said.
"There will be weddings," Ruth added.

They spoke of restoration. Of obedience rewarded. Of households realigned with God's will.

They were radiant.

In their minds, love had lost.

Religion had prevailed.

What they did not know—what no one outside the Harvey family knew—was that a message had already been sent.

Quietly.

Carefully.

The same afternoon the missionaries departed the ranch, Sam called for one of the ranch hands. There was no urgency in his voice, no drama. Just instruction.

"Ride into town," Sam said. "Find the women."

The ranch hand nodded, already mounting his horse.

"Tell them," Seth added, "that we ask them to come to dinner next Sunday. After church."

Silas spoke next. "They should bring their own wagons."

Saul's voice was steady. "They are to tell no one."

Scott added quietly, "Not the town."

Shane finished it. "Not the missionaries."

The ranch hand did not ask questions. He rode out as if it were an ordinary errand.

When he found the wives, he spoke plainly and without delay. There was no explanation beyond the invitation. No justification. Just the message.

The wives did not hesitate.

They did not ask why.

They did not ask what had changed.

They were thrilled—not desperate, not anxious, but glad.

Ada smiled first.
Ana laughed softly.
Asha closed her eyes in prayer.
Anne nodded once, already thinking through logistics.
Amy clasped her hands together.
Abby exhaled, joy rising like relief.

They prepared carefully.

Not nervously.

Not defensively.

They dressed beautifully.

Bright fabrics were chosen—colors that carried warmth and confidence. Dresses that moved easily, that allowed space for breath and motion. Boots polished. Jewelry selected with intention. Hair styled freely. Perfume worn lightly but without apology—the very thing the missionaries had always frowned upon.

Not as defiance.

As themselves.

They baked goods from their own ovens— warm bread, sweet rolls, cakes brushed with butter and glaze. Food made slowly, joyfully, by hands that believed nourishment was holy.

Sunday came.

Everyone attended church.

The men sat together, faces composed. The wives sat elsewhere, calm and dignified. The missionaries watched closely, already measuring posture and distance.

When the service ended, everyone left separately.

The men returned to the ranch first. They walked the familiar path with heavy steps— not from doubt, but from gravity. What they intended would change everything.

The wives arrived shortly after, wagons rolling up the drive quietly. Wheels crunched against gravel. Horses snorted softly. The air shifted as soon as they stepped down.

Then, at last, the missionaries arrived.

They came confident.

Smiling.

Already rehearsing their triumph.

When they saw the wives' wagons parked near the house, they exchanged glances of satisfaction.

"This is it," Clara whispered.

"They've accepted correction," Ruth murmured.

Inside the house, the Harvey brothers asked everyone to be seated in the parlor.

Chairs were arranged.

The wives sat together.

The missionaries positioned themselves across the room.

The air was thick, expectant.

Then, without warning or hesitation, the men stood.

Not all at once.

One by one.

Sam moved first.

He crossed the room slowly, deliberately, and knelt before Ada.

The missionaries stiffened.

Sam's voice did not shake.

"I am sorry," he said plainly. "For ever doubting the goodness of God in giving me you. For letting confusion speak louder than peace. For listening to voices that brought fear instead of life."

Ada did not speak. She placed her hands on his shoulders, eyes shining but steady.

Seth followed.

He knelt before Ana, head bowed.

"I missed you," he said simply. "I forgot what faith felt like without joy. Forgive me."

Ana's hands trembled as she lifted his face. "You are forgiven."

Silas knelt next.

Before Asha.

"For silence where I should have spoken," he said. "For allowing distance where there should have been unity."

Asha rested her forehead against his. "You came back."

Saul knelt before Anne.

"I let righteousness harden me," he said. "I forgot that love is not fragile."

Anne's eyes softened. "I knew you'd see."

Scott knelt before Amy.

"I confused restraint with holiness," he said. "And nearly lost what made me alive."

Amy laughed through tears. "You're here now."

Shane knelt last.

Before Abby.

"I almost believed God was disappointed in us," he admitted. "Forgive me."

Abby cupped his face. "God was never the one asking us to shrink."

Then the men stood.

Each one took his wife by the hands.

They lifted them up.

And they kissed them.

Openly.

Firmly.

Without shame.

In front of everyone present.

The wives did not shrink.

They kissed their husbands back—arms tight around them, joy unmistakable, covenant reclaimed in full view.

The room shattered.

"This is deception!" Eleanor shouted.

"You tricked us!" Clara cried.

Ruth's voice rose sharp and uncontrolled. "You are weak!"

"You chose lust over obedience!" Eleanor screamed.

The men did not respond.

The missionaries fled the house in fury and humiliation, skirts gathered, faces flushed, certainty collapsing behind them.

That night, the wives stayed.

The house filled again with warmth. With laughter. With shared food and presence. The men cooked. The women baked. Voices overlapped. Stories were told. The air breathed again.

What had been fractured was restored—not quietly, but clearly.

The men did not waver.

The wives did not gloat.

Covenant, once chosen again, needed no defense.

The next morning, the missionaries once gain met in their rooms.

And the Harvey household—tested by religion, strengthened by truth—stood whole, unashamed, and firmly joined, just as it had been meant to be.

Chapter 18

The missionaries did not give up.

They had never been women who surrendered easily, especially not when certainty had once lived so comfortably in their bones. If anything, what had happened at the Harvey Ranch only sharpened their resolve. In their minds, they had not lost. They had been *wronged.*

"That was deception," Clara said for the fifth time, pacing the narrow parlor of their room. "Calculated and Deliberate."

"They let us serve them," Ruth added, sitting stiff-backed at the table. "Sunday after Sunday."

"They ate our food," Eleanor said quietly, eyes narrowed. "They listened."

"And they gave us hope," Lydia said, voice trembling—not with sorrow, but with indignation.

Clara stopped pacing. "Exactly."

Eleanor folded her hands with purpose. "Good men do not allow women to serve them under false pretenses."

Ruth nodded vigorously. "It was an understanding."

Lydia hesitated. "It was... implied."

Eleanor's gaze snapped to her. "It was *clear*."

"They allowed us to believe," Clara continued, "that repentance was forming."

"That obedience was coming," Ruth said.

"That separation was imminent," Eleanor finished.

They all sat in silence for a moment, letting the outrage swell.

Then Clara smiled.

Not warmly.

Not kindly.

But decisively.

"We will seek justice."

Ruth straightened. "Civil justice."

Lydia blinked. "The court?"

"Of course the court," Clara replied. "God appoints authority."

Eleanor nodded. "And authority enforces order."

Ruth leaned forward. "We will accuse them of misconduct."

Lydia frowned. "Misconduct?"

"They accepted our service," Clara said. "That implies intention."

"They allowed emotional reliance," Ruth added. "Spiritual reliance."

"They led us on," Eleanor concluded.

Lydia swallowed. "They never promised—"

"They didn't *refuse*," Clara interrupted sharply.

That settled it.

By morning, they had a plan.

They dressed carefully—somber, respectable, righteous. Dresses pressed. Hair pinned tight. Bibles carried prominently, not to read, but to be seen. They walked into town together, heads high, expressions grave.

Their first stop was the sheriff's office.

Sheriff Dalton looked up from his desk, surprised to see six identical expressions of offense standing before him.

"Yes, ma'am?" he asked.

Eleanor stepped forward. "We wish to file a complaint."

Dalton leaned back. "Against whom?"

"The Harvey brothers," Clara said crisply.

Dalton blinked. "All six of 'em?"

"Yes," Ruth said.

"For what exactly?" he asked.

"They deceived us," Eleanor replied.

Dalton scratched his chin. "Deceived how?"

"They allowed us to serve them meals," Clara said solemnly.

Dalton paused. "That's... not illegal."

"They allowed us to believe," Ruth added, "that they intended to leave their wives."

Dalton raised an eyebrow. "Did they say that?"

"They implied it," Eleanor said firmly.

Dalton leaned forward. "Did they promise marriage?"

"No," Clara admitted.

"Did they promise divorce?" Dalton asked.

"No," Ruth said.

"Did they promise *anything*?" Dalton pressed.

They hesitated.

Lydia spoke softly. "They listened."

Dalton stared at them. "Listening isn't a crime."

Eleanor stiffened. "It is when it creates false hope."

Dalton sighed. "Ladies, hope ain't regulated by law."

Clara bristled. "We demand justice."

Dalton stood. "Justice for what?"

"For being led on," Ruth said.

"For emotional manipulation," Eleanor added.

"For allowing us to believe we were God's intended wives," Clara finished.

Dalton pinched the bridge of his nose. "I think you need to speak to the judge."

They left unsatisfied but undeterred.

Judge Whitcomb's office was quieter, heavier, lined with books and dust. The judge listened longer, hands folded, expression unreadable.

"You're saying," he summarized slowly, "that the Harvey men should be compelled by court order to divorce their wives."

"Yes," Eleanor said.

"And marry you," Ruth added.

"And remain with you for one year," Clara continued, "to perform missionary work."

The judge blinked.

Once.

Twice.

Then he leaned back.

"I've heard many things in this court," he said. "This is new."

"It's restitution," Eleanor insisted.

"They owe us," Clara said.

286

"For meals we cooked," Ruth added.

"For hope we invested," Lydia murmured.

The judge rubbed his temples. "You want me to order six married men to divorce their wives and remarry you?"

"Yes," Clara said confidently.

"For spiritual correction," Ruth added.

"And public example," Eleanor finished.

The judge stared at them for a long moment.

Then he laughed.

Not politely.

Not quietly.

He laughed until he had to remove his glasses and wipe his eyes.

"Ladies," he said finally, "this is not justice. This is lunacy."

Eleanor's face flushed. "You mock righteousness."

"No," the judge replied. "I protect sanity."

Clara stood. "We will appeal."

"To whom?" the judge asked.

"To God," Ruth said sharply.

The judge nodded. "I recommend prayer."

They left in fury.

Outside, Clara hissed, "The law is weak."

Eleanor's jaw tightened. "Then we will use reputation."

Ruth nodded. "Public accusation."

"They will crumble," Clara said. "Men always do."

Back at their lodging, they began writing again.

Letters to newspapers. Letters to church councils. Letters to distant boards.

They described betrayal.

They described manipulation.

They described themselves as victims of spiritual seduction.

They avoided facts.

They embellished feelings.

They framed hospitality as contract.

They framed silence as promise.

They framed kindness as obligation.

And they waited.

In Stillwater Crossing, the rumors tried to rise.

"They say the Harveys deceived them."

"They say the men led them on."

"They say the wives are manipulators."

The town listened.

Then looked around.

At the bakery feeding half the street.

At the market bustling on Saturdays.

At the amphitheater full of laughter.

At the Harvey men—working, faithful, steady.

At the wives—present, kind, unashamed.

Something didn't fit.

Sheriff Dalton said it plainly in the saloon one night. "If that's deception, then I've been deceived by pie."

Judge Whitcomb remarked to his wife, "If righteousness looks like that, I'd rather be corrected daily."

The missionaries waited for outrage.

They received amusement.

Clara slammed her letter down. "Why isn't this working?"

Eleanor's certainty cracked further. "Because they're laughing."

Ruth whispered, "They're not afraid."

Lydia sat quietly in the corner, finally asking the question that had been growing for months.

"What if," she said, "we were wrong?"

Silence.

Clara turned slowly. "Careful."

Eleanor stood. "Wrongness does not feel like this."

Lydia met her gaze. "Neither does God."

No one answered.

Outside, Stillwater Crossing continued to live.

And the missionaries—scheming, accusing, demanding—found themselves fighting something they had never learned how to defeat.

A community that had already moved on.

The women ask to come before once gain for justice.The judge did not laugh this time.

He sat back in his chair, fingers steepled, eyes fixed on the six missionary women standing before him. Sheriff Dalton stood to one side, arms crossed, expression no longer amused but sharpened with concern.

"Let me be very clear," Judge Whitcomb said slowly. "I need answers. Not Scripture. Not implication. Answers."

The room was silent.

Sheriff Dalton shifted his weight. "Ladies, the judge asked me to question you further before this goes any farther."

Eleanor lifted her chin. "We are prepared."

The judge nodded once. "Good. Then we'll begin."

He leaned forward.

"You are requesting that six legally married men be compelled by the court to divorce their wives."

"Yes," Eleanor said evenly.

"And that they then marry you."

"Yes," Clara added.

"And that this marriage," the judge continued, "would last for a full year."

"For missionary service," Ruth said quickly.

The judge paused. "Service."

"Yes," Eleanor confirmed.

Sheriff Dalton cleared his throat. "I'm going to ask this plainly."

They turned toward him.

"Are you asking the court to order these men into full marital relationships with you?"

There it was.

Silence stretched.

Clara spoke first. "We are asking for spiritual compensation."

Dalton frowned. "That's not what I asked."

Eleanor said, "Marriage is a spiritual institution."

Dalton nodded. "It's also a legal and physical one."

Ruth stiffened. "That aspect would be... restrained."

The judge raised an eyebrow. "Restrained how?"

"By discipline," Eleanor replied.

Dalton stepped closer. "So you're saying you expect six grown men to live as husbands in name only?"

Clara hesitated. "It would be understood—"

"Understood by whom?" Dalton pressed.

Eleanor's voice tightened. "By all parties."

The judge leaned back again. "You want me to order men into marriages where intimacy is prohibited?"

"Yes," Ruth said. "For holiness."

Dalton rubbed his jaw. "And what if it isn't prohibited?"

The missionaries froze.

Dalton continued, voice firm now. "What if children are conceived?"

Clara opened her mouth, then closed it.

The judge waited.

Eleanor spoke carefully. "That would be... unfortunate."

Dalton's eyes narrowed. "Unfortunate for who?"

"For the mission," Ruth said quietly.

"For the children?" Dalton asked.

Eleanor hesitated. "God provides for children."

The judge's voice hardened. "That's not an answer."

Dalton took another step. "Did you consider the human cost at all?"

Clara bristled. "We considered obedience."

Dalton snapped, "Obedience to whom?"

"To God," Eleanor said sharply.

The judge leaned forward, hands flat on the desk. "You are asking this court to override consent, covenant, affection, and bodily autonomy."

"It would be temporary," Clara insisted.

The judge stared at her. "Children are not temporary."

Silence.

Dalton pressed again. "Do you expect these men to love you?"

Ruth answered too quickly. "Love is learned."

Dalton shook his head slowly. "That's not how it works."

Eleanor said, "They were willing before."

Dalton snapped, "No, they weren't."

Clara's voice rose. "They allowed us to serve them."

Dalton shot back, "That's supper, not consent."

The judge held up a hand. "Enough."

He turned his gaze fully on Eleanor. "Let me ask you something very plainly."

She met his eyes.

"Do you believe these men want to be married to you?"

Eleanor's certainty faltered—just slightly. "They were confused."

The judge pressed. "That's not what I asked."

Ruth whispered, "They could be corrected."

The judge slammed his hand down—not hard, but final.

"This court does not correct men into marriages."

Dalton exhaled. "You're asking us to legislate desire."

Clara scoffed. "Desire is dangerous."

Dalton replied evenly, "So is power."

The judge stood.

"What you're describing," he said, "is not compensation. It is coercion."

Eleanor protested, "We were harmed."

The judge looked at her coldly. "You were disappointed."

Clara's voice shook. "We gave ourselves."

Dalton answered, "No one asked you to."

Ruth whispered, "They led us on."

The judge responded, "Listening is not a contract."

He moved around the desk now, standing closer to them.

"You did not consider children.
You did not consider consent.
You did not consider love.
You did not consider what marriage actually is."

Eleanor's voice hardened. "Marriage is obedience."

The judge shook his head. "Marriage is covenant."

Dalton added, "And covenant requires choice."

The judge stepped back. "This matter is closed."

Clara's face flushed with fury. "You're siding with sin."

The judge replied calmly, "I'm siding with reality."

Dalton opened the door. "Ladies."

They did not move at first.

Eleanor spoke one last time. "God will judge this."

The judge met her stare. "He already is."

As they left, the sheriff muttered under his breath, "Lord help us if that's righteousness."

When the door closed, the judge sank back into his chair.

"They never answered the question," Dalton said quietly.

"No," the judge replied. "Because the answer indicts them."

Dalton nodded. "They wanted religion without humanity."

The judge looked out the window toward town, toward the bakery, toward the life that continued.

"And that," he said, "is never justice."

Chapter 19

Terms, Interrogations, and the Anatomy of Delusion

The missionaries did not leave the courthouse relieved.

They left irritated.

Certainty, once cracked, does not disappear— it sharpens. It looks for new edges to cut with. And as the train tracks faded behind them and the rented parlor door shut, the question the judge had asked would not loosen its grip.

Intimacy.

It was the word they had avoided.
The word they had spiritualized away.
The word they now could not stop thinking about.

Clara broke the silence first, pacing again. "He trapped us with that question."

"No," Eleanor replied stiffly. "He forced us to be precise."

Ruth sat at the table, hands folded too tightly. "We should have been."

Lydia, quiet in the corner, did not speak.

Eleanor stopped pacing. "Let's be honest with ourselves."

Clara halted. "We are."

"No," Eleanor said. "We've been careful. That's not the same."

Ruth swallowed. "The judge asked what compensation meant."

"And we answered spiritually," Clara said.

"But he asked *humanly*," Eleanor replied.

Silence settled.

Then Ruth spoke, voice low. "We wanted what they have."

Clara's head snapped up. "That's not—"

"Yes," Ruth said, firmer now. "It is."

Eleanor's jaw tightened. "Say it plainly."

Ruth drew a breath. "We wanted the closeness. The attention. The affection."

Clara's voice wavered. "We wanted to be chosen."

Eleanor sat slowly. "We wanted marriage."

"Real marriage," Ruth added.

Lydia whispered from the corner, "Not ministry."

They all turned.

Lydia stood, hands shaking slightly. "You didn't want a year of prayer. You wanted the way those men looked at their wives."

No one contradicted her.

Clara sank into a chair. "The hugs."

"The kisses," Ruth said.

"The way they lean in," Clara added.

Eleanor closed her eyes briefly. "The warmth."

"And yes," Ruth continued, voice strained, "the physical part of marriage."

Lydia flinched. "Then say it."

Eleanor opened her eyes. "We will."

They sat down together and wrote.

Not Scripture.

Terms.

Divorce from current wives.
Immediate remarriage.
Duration: one year.

Affection daily.
Physical intimacy regularly.
Attention and companionship guaranteed.

They read it back to themselves.

"This is reasonable," Clara said, though her voice lacked conviction.

"This is compensation," Ruth insisted.

Eleanor nodded. "This is justice."

Lydia stared at the paper in horror. "This is delusion."

Clara snapped, "You're either with us or against us."

Lydia stood. "I'm with God."

Eleanor's voice hardened. "So are we."

They decided to escalate.

"If the judge refuses," Clara said, "we go higher."

"To the governor," Ruth added.

"And beyond," Eleanor said. "We start a campaign."

"For every Christian woman betrayed," Clara said.

"Every woman led on," Ruth added.

"Every woman replaced," Eleanor finished.

They believed themselves heroic.

They believed themselves righteous.

They did not see the unraveling.

Judge Whitcomb saw it immediately.

When the document reached his desk, he did not read it aloud. He read it once, slowly, then again, more carefully, his expression flattening with each line.

Sheriff Dalton watched him. "Well?"

The judge set the paper down as if it were something unstable. "They want the court to order affection."

Dalton blinked. "Affection."

"Kisses," the judge said. "Daily."

Dalton coughed. "Lord help us."

"And physical marriage," the judge continued. "Scheduled."

Dalton leaned back. "That's... ambitious."

The judge removed his glasses. "That's delusional."

Dalton nodded. "That's what I was afraid of."

The judge stood and walked to the window. "I will not have my jurisdiction turned into a spectacle."

"What now?" Dalton asked.

The judge turned. "Now I interrogate."

Dalton raised an eyebrow. "Who first?"

"The men," the judge said. "Alone."

"And the wives?"

"After," the judge replied. "They deserve to hear this clearly."

He sighed. "I want truth, not theater."

The Harvey brothers were summoned the next morning.

They entered the judge's chambers together, hats in hand, expressions wary but steady.

The judge gestured to the chairs. "Sit."

They sat.

"I'm going to ask you some questions," he said. "Answer plainly."

Sam nodded. "Yes, sir."

The judge leaned forward. "Did you promise these women marriage?"

"No," Sam said.

"Did you promise divorce?"

"No."

"Did you promise affection?"

Seth blinked. "No, sir."

The judge nodded. "Did you want to marry them?"

Silence.

Then Saul spoke. "No."

Scott added, "Never."

Shane said quietly, "We were confused. Not consenting."

The judge exhaled. "Did you want intimacy with them?"

All six men shook their heads.

The judge leaned back. "That is sufficient."

Dalton opened the door. "Bring in the wives."

The women entered together.

The judge stood when they did. "Thank you for coming."

Ada inclined her head. "Of course."

"I will be direct," the judge said. "The missionaries have submitted terms."

Anne crossed her arms. "Terms."

"Yes," he said. "They want me to order your husbands into marriages with them. Full marriages."

Abby laughed once. "That's rich."

The judge raised a hand. "Including affection, intimacy, and attention by schedule."

Amy's smile vanished. "They want ownership."

Ana said quietly, "They want what they cannot compel."

Asha spoke softly. "This is not faith."

The judge nodded. "I agree."

He turned to the men. "Do any of you want this?"

Six voices answered together. "No."

The judge folded his hands. "Then we are done."

He stood, authority filling the room.

"This court will not order affection.
It will not command intimacy.
It will not dissolve covenant for desire dressed as righteousness."

Dalton opened the door again. "Bring in the missionaries."

They entered confident.

They left pale.

The judge read their terms aloud.

The room went very quiet.

"This," he said, holding up the paper, "is not compensation."

He met Eleanor's eyes. "This is obsession."

Clara protested, "We were wronged."

The judge replied evenly, "You were disappointed."

Ruth cried, "We gave everything."

The judge answered, "No one asked you to give desire."

He leaned forward. "This matter ends today."

Eleanor's voice shook. "We will go to the governor."

The judge nodded. "You may."

"But you will not turn my court into a stage."

Dalton added dryly, "We already have an amphitheater for that."

The wives did not speak.

They did not need to.

The madness had been exposed.

And Stillwater Crossing, spared spectacle, returned to life—wiser, steadier, and no longer confused about the difference between faith and fixation.

Chapter 20

The Signs, the Names, and the Week That Felt Like a Year

By the time the missionaries began picketing the bakery, obsession had fully taken hold.

It was no longer subtle.
It was no longer quiet.
And it was certainly no longer dignified.

They arrived just after sunrise, six of them, dressed in their familiar dark clothing, hair pinned tight, faces set with a fervor that startled the milkman so badly he nearly dropped his cans.

They carried signs.

Large signs.

Signs that had clearly taken time, ink, and far too much conviction.

One read:

JILTED IN THE NAME OF GOD

Another:

**UNSANCTIONED WIVES.
UNSANCTIONED BEDS.**

A third, written in block letters so sharp they looked angry:

THESE WOMEN STOLE OUR HUSBANDS

Abby stopped short when she saw them through the bakery window.

"Well," she said mildly, "they've escalated."

Anne adjusted her glasses and read another sign aloud.

FULL MARITAL RIGHTS DENIED TO GODLY WOMEN

Amy blinked. "Did they... did they write that?"

Ana crossed herself instinctively. "Sweet Jesus."

Asha closed her eyes. "Lord, restrain them."

The missionaries positioned themselves directly in front of the bakery entrance.

"Shame!" Clara called out as the first customer approached.

"God sees!" Ruth added.

"Repent!" Eleanor cried, lifting her sign higher.

The customer—a farmer's wife who had come every morning for fresh bread—froze.

"I just wanted a loaf," she said uncertainly.

"You are complicit," Clara told her solemnly.

The woman squinted. "In bread?"

"IN SIN," Ruth corrected.

The woman turned slowly and walked away.

Inside the bakery, Amy exhaled. "They're harassing customers."

Anne nodded. "Document everything."

Abby peeked again through the window. "They're chanting."

Indeed, they were.

"ONE YEAR FOR THE LORD!"
"ONE YEAR FOR THE LORD!"

Hannah arrived not long after, basket on her arm.

She took one look, raised an eyebrow, and said calmly, "Well. That's unfortunate."

"Do we say something?" Abby asked.

Hannah shook her head. "No."

311

Anne looked surprised. "None of us?"

"No," Hannah repeated. "We pray."

They prayed.

Not loudly.

Not theatrically.

They prayed while kneading dough.
While sweeping floors.
While tying aprons.

Outside, the missionaries grew louder.

"THEY SLEEP WITH OUR HUSBANDS!" one
of them shouted.

A passerby stopped short. "I beg your
pardon?"

"They are fulfilling wifely duties unsanctioned
by God!" Clara announced.

The man stared. "That's... that's what wives
do."

"NOT WITHOUT APPROVAL," Ruth
snapped.

By midday, the sheriff arrived.

Sheriff Dalton took in the scene slowly—the signs, the chanting, the increasingly confused townspeople.

"Ladies," he said evenly, "you're obstructing business."

"We are proclaiming truth," Eleanor replied.

"You're harassing customers," Dalton said.

"They're supporting adultery," Clara shot back.

Dalton sighed. "No, ma'am. They're buying bread."

The missionaries did not disperse.

They doubled down.

They began introducing themselves to anyone who would listen.

"We are Mrs. Harvey," Ruth said proudly to a curious woman.

Dalton froze. "Excuse me?"

"By faith," Eleanor added quickly.

"By delusion," Dalton muttered under his breath.

News traveled fast.

By the next morning, a reporter from the local paper arrived, notebook in hand.

"So," he said, pen poised, "you're claiming these men are your husbands?"

"In spirit," Clara replied.

"And in destiny," Ruth added.

"And in law?" the reporter asked.

Eleanor hesitated. "Soon."

The headline the next day read:

SIX WOMEN CLAIM HARVEY NAME, DEMAND COURT-ORDERED AFFECTION

The town erupted.

By midweek, women from neighboring towns arrived.

Some stood with the missionaries.

Single women. Bitter women. Women who had been disappointed once and never forgiven the world for it.

Others stood with the Stage Six.

Married women. Working women. Women who had watched the bakery feed their children and the market revive their streets.

The street outside the bakery turned into a debate ground.

"This is about godliness!" a missionary supporter shouted.

"This is about obsession!" a farmer's wife yelled back.

"You're jealous!" someone accused.

"Of WHAT?" Abby shouted, unable to stop herself.

Hannah gently touched her arm. "Still. We pray."

Inside his chambers, Judge Whitcomb rubbed his temples.

"This has gone too far," he said.

Dalton nodded. "They're calling themselves Harvey now."

The judge groaned. "I knew it."

"They're blocking commerce," Dalton added. "Harassment. Public disturbance."

The judge stood. "Draft a warning."

By afternoon, Dalton delivered it.

"Ladies," he announced, "you are ordered to cease picketing immediately or face arrest."

Eleanor lifted her chin. "We are martyrs."

Dalton replied flatly, "You are trespassing."

The judge sent a telegram that same day.

The mission board was notified.

SEND REPRESENTATIVES IMMEDIATELY. SITUATION UNSTABLE.

The reply came back swiftly.

TWO REPRESENTATIVES EN ROUTE. ARRIVAL IN ONE WEEK.

When the missionaries learned of it, they panicked.

"They're coming to remove us," Clara hissed.

"We can't leave like this," Ruth said.

"We need victory," Eleanor insisted.

They escalated again.

Bigger signs.
Louder chants.
More accusations.

They followed customers down the street.

They interrupted conversations.

They prayed loudly, dramatically, theatrically—hands raised, voices shaking.

Newspapers from neighboring towns picked up the story.

RELIGIOUS WOMEN DEMAND COURT-ORDERED MARRIAGE

BAKERY AT CENTER OF MORAL STANDOFF

By Friday, Judge Whitcomb had had enough.

He drafted restraining orders.

"They will not come within fifty yards of the bakery, the market, or the ranch," he said.

"Until the mission representatives arrive."

Dalton nodded. "About time."

When the order was served, the missionaries screamed.

"This is persecution!" Clara cried.

"This is injustice!" Ruth shouted.

"This is God testing us!" Eleanor declared.

Hannah watched from across the street, calm.

"They are unraveling," Anne said quietly.

"Yes," Hannah replied. "And being seen."

The Stage Six continued working.

They baked.
They sold.
They built.

They did not argue.

They did not confront.

They prayed.

By the time the train carrying the mission representatives was due, the entire region knew the story.

And by then, it was no longer confusing who was standing in truth.

The week felt like a year.

But it ended.

And when it did, Stillwater Crossing would finally exhale—leaving behind the madness, the signs, and the mistaken belief that obsession could ever be mistaken for faith.

Chapter 21

What Took Root and What Was Carried

The mission representatives arrived on a quiet morning.

No banners.
No hymns.
No spectacle.

Just two people stepping off the train—one man, one woman—both dressed plainly, both carrying the unmistakable look of people who had been sent to clean up a mess rather than celebrate a victory.

They did not go first to the bakery.

They went to the courthouse.

Judge Whitcomb received them with measured relief.

"We apologize," the woman said immediately, removing her gloves. "For the confusion. For the disruption. For the distress caused to this town."

The man beside her nodded. "This should never have reached this point."

Sheriff Dalton folded his arms. "That's putting it mildly."

They apologized again—to the judge, to the sheriff, to the town council.

They did **not** apologize to the six missionary women.

Instead, they asked to meet with them privately at the church.

The meeting lasted less than an hour.

When the door opened, the outcome was written plainly on faces.

The mission representative spoke first. "You are required to repent."

Clara laughed, sharp and hollow.
Ruth crossed her arms.
Eleanor lifted her chin.

"We have nothing to repent of," Eleanor said.

The man's voice was steady. "Obsession is not zeal."

"This town corrupted us," Clara snapped.

"No," the woman replied calmly. "You abandoned restraint."

They were offered counseling.
They were offered removal.
They were offered a return east.

All refused.

All except Lydia.

She stood shaking, eyes red, voice barely holding.

"I am sorry," she said. "To God. To them. To myself."

The other five turned on her instantly.

"Traitor."
"You loved men more than God."
"You were weak."

Lydia did not answer.

She simply wept.

Later the wives heard what had happened to Lydia. They quickly found out where she was and before she left and they stepped forward.

Ada spoke first. "Do you need work?"

Lydia looked up, stunned. "I—what. yes?"

Anne added, "And a place to live."

Amy smiled gently. "We have room at the boardinghouse."

Abby tilted her head. "No sermons required."

Asha said softly, "Only honesty."

The other missionaries had heard about their offer to Lydia and gasped.

"The wives would take *her* in?" Clara cried.

"She betrayed us!"

Lydia stayed.

The other five left town under escort, furious and unrepentant, certainty intact but credibility gone.

Stillwater Crossing exhaled.

What followed did not look like revival.

It looked like life.

The bakery expanded first.

New ovens were installed. Morning lines formed. Children ran errands eagerly. Amy's laugh became as familiar as the smell of bread.

The sewing center opened next.

Ada and Anne ran it together—precision and numbers married to dignity and speed. Women learned trades. Dresses were altered. Curtains sewn. Confidence tailored stitch by stitch.

The farmers market came alive on Saturdays.

Produce. Eggs. Honey. Music drifting between stalls. No gatekeeping. No sermons shouted. Just presence.

Then the amphitheater.

Simple wood. Open sky.

On market days, the Stage Six danced.

For free.

Or for contributions tossed into baskets by laughing children and generous farmers.

They danced joy.

They danced healing.

They danced stories.

People came from neighboring towns—not to protest, but to watch.

Lydia found her place quietly.

She worked the books. She learned. She listened. She healed in anonymity, grateful beyond words.

And then—because life insists on its own humor—

They all got pregnant.

Not one by one.

Together.

The town did not know what to do with that.

The dancing continued.

Up to nine months.

The steps changed.

Slower turns. Wider stances. Careful spins.

Abby called it "expectant choreography."

Amy nearly fell laughing the first time they practiced.

"You realize," she said between breaths, "no one has ever choreographed for six pregnant women at once."

"Then we're pioneers," Anne replied.

They danced until the very end.

The men watched from the sidelines—proud, bewildered, deeply in love.

Children were born into laughter.

Into bread and music and work.

Into a town that had learned—slowly, painfully—that holiness does not strangle life.

It feeds it.

And Stillwater Crossing, once nearly undone by religion, became known for something else entirely:

A place where covenant held.
Where joy was not suspicious.
Where love was not rationed.
Where truth, once revealed, was allowed to live.

That was the year everything changed.

Not because someone won.

But because love refused to be divided.

Epilogue Scriptures — "What Love Built"

On Covenant That Cannot Be Divided
"What therefore God has joined together, let not man separate."
— **Mark 10:9**

"Though one may be overpowered, two can defend themselves. A cord of three strands is not quickly broken."
— **Ecclesiastes 4:12**

On Love as the Measure of Faith
"A new commandment I give to you, that you love one another: just as I have loved you."
— **John 13:34**

"By this all people will know that you are my disciples, if you have love for one another."
— **John 13:35**

"If I have all faith so as to remove mountains, but have not love, I am nothing."
— **1 Corinthians 13:2**

On Religion Without Love Being Empty
"Having a form of godliness but denying its power. Have nothing to do with such people."
— **2 Timothy 3:5**

"The letter kills, but the Spirit gives life."
— **2 Corinthians 3:6**

On Fruit as the Evidence of Truth
"By their fruit you will recognize them."
— **Matthew 7:16**

"The fruit of the Spirit is love, joy, peace, patience, kindness, goodness, faithfulness."
— **Galatians 5:22**

"A good tree cannot bear bad fruit, and a bad tree cannot bear good fruit."
— **Matthew 7:18**

On Freedom, Not Fear
"For God has not given us a spirit of fear, but of power, love, and a sound mind."
— **2 Timothy 1:7**

"It is for freedom that Christ has set us free."
— **Galatians 5:1**

On Building That Lasts
"Unless the Lord builds the house, the builders labor in vain."
— **Psalm 127:1**

"They will rebuild the ancient ruins and restore the places long devastated."
— **Isaiah 61:4**

On Hospitality and Shared Life
"They broke bread in their homes and ate together with glad and sincere hearts."
— **Acts 2:46**

"Do not forget to show hospitality to strangers, for by so doing some people have shown hospitality to angels without knowing it."
— **Hebrews 13:2**

On Joy That Is Not a Sin
"The joy of the Lord is your strength."
— **Nehemiah 8:10**

"There is a time to dance."
— **Ecclesiastes 3:4**

On Children as Blessing, Not Consequence
"Children are a heritage from the Lord, offspring a reward from him."
— **Psalm 127:3**

"You shall be blessed more than any other people."
— **Deuteronomy 7:14**

On Truth Standing Without Force
"Not by might nor by power, but by my Spirit, says the Lord Almighty."
— **Zechariah 4:6**

"You will know the truth, and the truth will set you free."
— **John 8:32**

Closing Scripture for the Final Page

"Let all that you do be done in love."
— **1 Corinthians 16:14**

Book Club Discussion Questions — "What Love Built"

Section 1: Covenant vs. Control

Mark 10:9 | Ecclesiastes 4:12

1. Where in the story did you see covenant tested most severely, and what ultimately held it together?
2. Have you ever witnessed or experienced a situation where people tried to "divide" what God had joined? What language was used to justify it?
3. How does the novel challenge the idea that marriage or covenant requires approval beyond God Himself?
4. What does a "cord of three strands" look like practically in relationships—marriage, friendship, or community?

Section 2: Love as the True Measure of Faith

John 13:34–35 | 1 Corinthians 13:2

5. How did the characters demonstrate love without needing permission or validation?
6. Which moments showed love *before* theology or rules?
7. How does the novel confront the idea that correct belief matters more than loving action?
8. In your own life, where has love been replaced with performance, fear, or approval-seeking?

Section 3: When Religion Loses Its Power

2 Timothy 3:5 | 2 Corinthians 3:6

9. What signs in the story showed "a form of godliness" without spiritual life?
10. How did religious language become a tool rather than a source of healing?
11. Have you ever seen Scripture used to restrict rather than restore?
12. What is the difference between discipline that gives life and control that drains it?

Section 4: Fruit as Evidence

Matthew 7:16–18 | Galatians 5:22

13. What fruit did each group produce—peace or fear, life or division?
14. How did the businesses, families, and community reflect spiritual fruit more clearly than sermons?
15. Which fruits of the Spirit were most visible by the end of the novel?
16. Why do you think fruit is a better measure of truth than intention?

Section 5: Freedom vs. Fear

2 Timothy 1:7 | Galatians 5:1

17. Where did fear first begin to influence decisions in the story?
18. How did freedom look different from rebellion in the wives' choices?
19. What fears are most often disguised as "wisdom" or "discernment" in religious spaces today?
20. In what ways does fear try to masquerade as holiness?

Section 6: Building What Lasts

Psalm 127:1 | Isaiah 61:4

21. What did the characters build that outlasted opposition?
22. How does the novel redefine "success" in building community?
23. Why is restoration often quieter—and more powerful—than reform?
24. What "ruins" do you think God is still rebuilding through ordinary faithfulness?

Section 7: Hospitality, Joy, and Daily Life

Acts 2:46 | Hebrews 13:2 | Ecclesiastes 3:4

25. How did shared meals and work become sacred spaces in the story?
26. Why do you think joy and dancing were treated as threats by some characters?
27. What does the novel teach about joy as a spiritual discipline?
28. Where have you seen hospitality change hearts more than arguments?

Section 8: Children, Legacy, and Multiplication

Psalm 127:3 | Deuteronomy 7:14

29. How did the ending redefine "blessing" beyond material or moral success?
30. What does generational blessing look like when rooted in love rather than control?
31. How do children in the story represent fruit rather than reward?

Section 9: Truth Without Force

Zechariah 4:6 | John 8:32

32.   How did truth prevail without shouting, debating, or winning arguments?

33.   What role did patience play in exposing deception?

34.   Why do you think truth often reveals itself over time rather than instantly?

35.   What does this story suggest about God's role versus human effort in resolving conflict?

Closing Reflection

1 Corinthians 16:14

36.   Looking back over the entire novel, what does it mean to you now to "let all that you do be done in love"?

37.   How has this story challenged or affirmed your understanding of faith, marriage, community, or calling?

38.   What is one belief, habit, or fear this book invites you to release?

How to Start a Farmers Market (1890s-Inspired, Still Works Today)

A farmer's market is not merely commerce. It is community made visible.

Step 1: Begin with Purpose

Decide why the market exists.

- To feed families
- To support local growers and bakers
- To create gathering, not competition
- To restore dignity through honest work

Write this purpose down. Let it guide decisions.

Step 2: Secure a Simple Location

Look for:

- Open land near town
- A wide street, green, or shared commons
- Proximity to foot traffic

It does not need to be grand. It must be accessible.

Step 3: Invite Producers, Not Vendors

Start with people who already produce:

- Farmers
- Bakers
- Egg sellers
- Soap or candle makers
- Seamstresses
- Herbalists

Encourage *local first*. Keep costs low or contribution-based.

Step 4: Establish Clear, Gentle Rules

- No price gouging
- No exclusivity
- No shaming
- No political or religious coercion

Let quality and kindness regulate the space.

Step 5: Make It Relational

- Encourage shared meals
- Allow music or dancing
- Welcome children
- Let people linger

A market thrives when people feel seen.

Step 6: Keep the Spirit Open

Prayer may happen.
So may laughter.
So may questions.

Do not force meaning.
Let fruit speak.

How to Start a Book Club

A book club is a circle, not a classroom.

Step 1: Choose the Right Environment

- Homes
- Bakeries
- Community rooms
- Market spaces after hours

Comfort invites honesty.

Step 2: Set the Tone Early

State clearly:

- No one must agree
- No one must perform faith
- Questions are welcome
- Silence is allowed

Trust grows where pressure is absent.

Step 3: Read With Curiosity, Not Defense

Encourage members to ask:

- What moved me?
- What unsettled me?
- What do I recognize in myself?

Not: "What is the correct answer?"

Step 4: Let Scripture Be Companion, Not Weapon

Use Scripture to reflect, not to correct.
Invite insight.
Do not demand conclusion.

Step 5: Close With Gratitude

End meetings by naming:

- One truth learned
- One moment of connection
- One question worth holding

Growth often begins with what we do not yet resolve.

The Sinner's Prayer (Invitation, Not Formula)

This prayer is not magic.
It is surrender.

Prayer
Lord Jesus,
I come to You honestly.
I believe You are the Son of God.
I believe You lived, died, and rose again for me.
I confess my need for You.
I turn from sin, fear, and self-rule.
I receive Your forgiveness.
I receive Your life.
Teach me to love as You love.
I place my trust in You.
Amen.

What to Do After the Prayer Is Prayed

Salvation begins a walk—it does not end a journey.

1. Rest

Do not rush to fix yourself.
Grace works inward before it shows outward.

2. Read Scripture Slowly

Begin with:

- The Gospel of John
- Psalms
- Romans 8

Read to listen, not to master.

3. Pray Honestly

Speak plainly.
God already knows.

4. Find Safe Community

Look for people who:

- Bear fruit
- Practice humility
- Love without control

Avoid environments built on fear.

5. Let Change Be Organic

Transformation is fruit, not performance.
Growth happens as love deepens.

A Healing Prayer (Body, Soul, and Memory)

This prayer may be spoken aloud or quietly.

Healing Prayer
Lord Jesus,
You are the Healer of all things.
I bring You my body, my heart, my memories,
and my wounds.
Where there is pain, bring Your peace.
Where there is fear, bring Your presence.
Where there is sickness, bring Your healing
power.
I ask You to touch what I cannot reach
and restore what I cannot repair.
I receive Your mercy without shame
and Your healing without striving.
Let Your life flow through me.
Amen.

Final Note to the Reader

Faith that cannot dance, feed, build, or heal
is not the faith Jesus taught.

Love is the measure.
Fruit is the evidence.
And covenant—when chosen freely—creates
life.

Stage Six Bakery Recipes 1890s

1. Hearth-Baked White Bread (Everyday Loaf)

Ingredients
4 cups bread flour
1 cup warm milk
1 cup warm water
2 tablespoons lard or butter
2 tablespoons sugar
1 tablespoon salt
1 cake compressed yeast (or 2¼ tsp active dry yeast)

Method
Dissolve yeast in warm water with sugar. Let stand until foamy. Stir in milk, melted fat, and salt. Work in flour gradually until a soft dough forms. Knead by hand 10–15 minutes until elastic. Place in greased bowl, cover, and let rise until doubled. Shape into loaves, place in pans, rise again. Bake in a moderate oven (375°F) 35–40 minutes until golden and hollow-sounding.

Use in Bakery: Daily staple, sandwich bread, church loaves.

2. Molasses Oat Bread

Ingredients
2 cups rolled oats
2 cups boiling water
3 cups flour
½ cup molasses
2 tablespoons butter
1 teaspoon salt
1 cake yeast dissolved in ½ cup warm water

Method
Pour boiling water over oats and butter; cool to warm. Stir in molasses, salt, and yeast. Add flour gradually. Knead lightly. Let rise until doubled. Shape into loaves and bake at 375°F for 40 minutes.

Flavor: Hearty, slightly sweet, filling.

3. Apple Hand Pies (Railway Favorite)

Ingredients
4 cups chopped dried apples (soaked overnight)
½ cup sugar
1 teaspoon cinnamon
¼ teaspoon nutmeg
Pastry dough (lard crust recommended)

Method
Simmer apples with sugar and spices until thick. Roll pastry thin, cut circles, fill, fold, crimp. Bake hot (400°F) until browned.

Sold wrapped in paper for travelers.

4. Cornmeal Drop Cakes

Ingredients
1 cup cornmeal
1 cup flour
½ cup sugar
1 cup milk
1 egg
1 tablespoon melted butter
1 teaspoon baking soda

Method
Mix dry ingredients. Stir in milk, egg, and butter. Drop by spoonfuls onto greased pans. Bake 375°F for 15–18 minutes.

Popular with children and farmers.

5. Gingerbread Loaf (No Frosting)

Ingredients
2 cups flour
1 cup molasses

½ cup lard or butter
1 cup hot water
1 teaspoon soda
1 teaspoon ginger
½ teaspoon cloves
½ teaspoon cinnamon
½ teaspoon salt

Method
Cream fat and molasses. Dissolve soda in hot water. Combine all ingredients. Pour into pan. Bake at 350°F for 45 minutes.

Keeps well; improves with age.

6. Lard Crust Pie Dough (Foundation Recipe)

Ingredients
3 cups flour
1 teaspoon salt
1¼ cups lard
Cold water as needed

Method
Cut lard into flour and salt until pea-sized. Add water sparingly. Handle lightly. Chill before rolling.

Used for fruit pies, meat pies, custards.

7. Peach Cobbler (Market Day Special)

Ingredients
6 cups sliced peaches
1 cup sugar
1 cup flour
1 cup milk
1 teaspoon baking powder
¼ cup butter

Method
Melt butter in baking dish. Mix flour, sugar, baking powder, milk. Pour over butter. Add peaches. Bake 375°F until bubbling and browned.

Served warm with cream.

8. Pound Cake (Bakery Pride Cake)

Ingredients
1 pound butter
1 pound sugar
1 pound eggs
1 pound flour
1 teaspoon lemon zest

Method
Cream butter and sugar thoroughly. Add eggs one at a time. Fold in flour and zest. Bake slowly at 325°F in greased pans.

Celebration cake; sliced thick.

9. Honey Drop Biscuits

Ingredients
2 cups flour
1 tablespoon baking powder
$\frac{1}{2}$ teaspoon salt
2 tablespoons honey
1 cup milk
2 tablespoons butter

Method
Mix dry ingredients. Stir in milk, honey, butter. Drop onto pan. Bake 400°F for 12–15 minutes.

Excellent with ham or preserves.

10. Fruitcake for Keeping (Christmas or Rail Shipping)

Ingredients
2 cups flour
1 cup butter
1 cup sugar
4 eggs
2 cups mixed dried fruit
$\frac{1}{2}$ cup nuts
1 teaspoon cinnamon
$\frac{1}{2}$ teaspoon cloves
$\frac{1}{4}$ cup brandy or cider (optional)

Method
Cream butter and sugar. Add eggs. Stir in fruit, nuts, spices, flour. Bake low and slow at 300°F for 2½ hours. Wrap and store.

A symbol of prosperity and endurance.

www.ingramcontent.com/pod-product-compliance
Lightning Source LLC
Chambersburg PA
CBHW050920030726
47503CB00007BB/2391